# GET ME OUT OF WITCH SCHOOL!

# EM LYNAS

illustrated by JAMIE LITTLER

nosy
crow

To my big kids,
Katherine and Christopher.
You are the Best
and Brightest.
x

E. L.

First published in the UK in 2018 by Nosy Crow Ltd
The Crow's Nest, 14 Baden Place, Crosby Row
London, SE1 1YW, UK

Nosy Crow and associated logos are trademarks and/or registered
trademarks of Nosy Crow Ltd

Text copyright © Em Lynas, 2018
Cover and illustrations copyright © Jamie Littler, 2018
Cover title typography © Thomas Flintham, 2018

A CIP catalogue record for this book will be available from the British Library.

Printed and bound in the UK by Clays Ltd, St. Ives Plc

Papers used by Nosy Crow are made from wood grown in
sustainable forests.

ISBN: 978 1 7880 0038 3

www.nosycrow.com

**TWINKLE TOADSPIT** is a
Shakespearean actress AND a mega-witch
BUT she must get out of witch school or her
Bottom is DOOMED!

***Summary:***

*This is the current situation I am currently experiencing in my current location.*

I am walking through the corridors of Toadspit Towers, Witch School of Conformity and Strictness, with my friends. Shalini is being quiet and Jess is not. We are all first-year witches and we share a dormitory with Dominique and Arwen, who are not my friends. They are nowhere to be seen. I am not suspecting invisibility. Just absence. Which is a good thing because Dominique, who is usually the Best and Brightest witch of Toadspit Towers, has not reacted well to my new-found witchiness.

We're on our way to the dining hall for tea and I

am not anticipating food of deliciousness for I have earned NO TICKS today and NO TICKS means NO FOOD. Just GLOOP. This is not a treat for the tastebuds.

Jess is bouncing, no, bounding along in front of me. Her tie's loose, her short brown hair, bobbed with a fringe, hasn't been brushed at the back and her shirt is hanging out. She's enjoying the absence of the "Tidy and Trim" Toadspit rule now that there are no rules at all. Even her hat, splodges of every shade of green, looks messier. The feather and bow are flipping and flopping with each enthusiastic bound. She's like a puppy!

Shalini is walking. She is tidy and trim. Her long black hair is in a neat plait and everything is tied and tucked in properly. Her green hat is different shades of green too, because they are both first-generation witches, but her greens blend together like a field of Granny's nettles at sunset.

There's a big grin on Jess's round face and I am beginning to wonder if someone has cast a chatterbox

spell on her, if there is such a thing. Which I would not know because, as has been stated today by Ms

Thorn, Deputy Headmistress of Toadspit Towers, I am currently demonstrating IGNORANCE and she has banned me from performing any sort of unsupervised magic until I have been TRAINED and EDUCATED. Thus avoiding magical mayhem, catastrophic consequences and the destruction of the school. Those are her words, not mine.

Jess twizzles round to face me.

"Do you mind that you killed your great-great-great-great-grandmother?" she asks.

"Jess!" That's Shalini.

"I did not kill Ursula Toadspit! She was already dead." That's me.

"Deceased her then," says Jess, as we reach a set of creaky stairs. "After all, you *did* break the curse her daughter, Marietta Toadspit, had placed upon her. Ms Ursula *did* stop haunting her doll and ruling the school. You *did* reveal your witch's hat of awesomeness and you *did* inherit Toadspit Towers and everything in it. Is this correct?"

Obviously, it's completely correct, but it sounds

bad for Greats-Grandma Ursula, even though it was a good thing that she was released from the Toadspit Curse.

"So now you actually own this whole wall," says Jess, sweeping her arm across the stone blocks. "And this wonky picture." She straightens the picture of an old witch peering into a cauldron. "And these stairs!" The feather in her hat flicks up and down as she jumps from step to step all the way to the bottom. "And this bannister and this door and this door knob and these hinges and this gargoyle." The gargoyle knocker on the door grunts at her and sticks its tongue out.

Jess has been talking and asking questions all the way from our Pottering With Potions lesson, which was a disaster, and I have been trying to ignore her because I am ac-chew-ally attempting to ponder on the PROBLEM OF ENORMITY that is now my life. In the last two days I have made DISCOVERIES. I have thought of QUESTIONS. I have NO ANSWERS.

★

*Discovery 1: Even though I am officially IGNORANT I am ac-chew-ally a mega witch of mega power. A seventh of seven witch with a Rainbow Hat of Awesomeness. The only seventh of seven witch in the school. I am unique.*

*Discovery 2: I am ac-chew-ally part witchwood. My left thumb is now not made of me.*

*Discovery 3: I am ac-chew-ally the descendent of Ms Ursula Toadspit, founder of Toadspit Towers. Which means Jess is right. I do, technically, own the school but not until I come of age. That age is eighteen. Not eleven.*

Jess interrupts my thoughts as she jump-stamps. "You own this floorboard and this floorboard and this floorboard and this floorboard and—"

Shalini's had enough too. "Stop stamping! I think she knows!"

I continue to ignore her and continue to ponder as

we continue to walk through the school.

*Question 1: Am I an actresswitch or a witchactress? Or a witress? A witchess, or an actritch?*

*Question 2: Would it be fair to use my witchy skills to be a better actress and get an Oscar before I am twelve years old? Would that be considered cheating?*

*Question 3: What exactly are my witchy powers? I have failed every task Ms Thorn has set me so far even though I got every single witch assessment right on my first day. But that was because the witchwood was helping. And now it is not allowed to help because that is definitely cheating.*

*Answers: As previously mentioned – I have none.*

*Plans: I have none.*

I'm now pondering about last night. Last night was

the best night of my entire acting career. My Bottom was outstanding. In fact, Mr Marlow, my acting teacher, said it was the best Bottom performance in any *Midsummer Night's Dream* he had ever seen and he's seen a lot of Bottom performances at St Bluebottle's School of Creativity and Fun, which is my old school. But what I am currently thinking is *What if I never get to act again? What if my acting career is over? What if I am now just a witch?*

*I would be living in an ac-chew-al TRAGEDY OF DESPAIR!*

"And you've inherited all of the Toadspit magical powers!" says Jess. "All of Ms Toadspit's memories were zapped into your head and now it's like—"

"An encyclopedia of magical knowledge," says Shalini. "All in one head."

Now her eyes are sparkling and her hat-light is shining down from the brim, lighting up her face.

I attempt to sidestep them both as I say, "I am not an encyclopedia. I told you. Grandma Ursula's memories fizzed into my mind just before she deceased, but they disappeared. Like when a bubble bursts and leaves a watermark then it dries up and it's like it never, ever existed. Which is why I am annoying Ms Thorn with my zero magical knowledge."

I attempt another sidestep, between Jess and the wall.

Jess gasps in that way a person gasps when they think they've had an idea of brilliance.

"But, Twink! What if the memories are just buried? In the furthest reaches of your mind. I could hypnotise you. I once hypnotised my mam and she remembered where she'd left Grandma. If I hypnotised you I could release Ms Toadspit's memories. We could find out why Marietta cursed her mother to be headmistress until another Toadspit arrived and broke all the rules. We could uncover the truth!"

I give Jess my firm and forceful look. "Jess. You are not going to hypnotise me. There are no memories to find. They ... popped!"

"Hm." She leans towards me and I lean back against the wall, pressing my hands on the rough

stone. "Are you sure?" she says.

"Shush," I say.

Jess does not comply. She keeps talking. "There was the case of Ms Willowslime and the lost crystal plum. She—"

I shush her again.

"Stop shushing me," says Jess.

I shush her again.

"Can you hear that?" I say.

"Hear what?" says Shalini. She does a look from *The Book of Listening Curiously.*

Jess also says, "Hear what?"

"That!" I say.

I am hearing a noise. A whispering noise. I listen harder. It isn't coming from anyone in the corridor. The corridor is empty. It's coming from the wall behind me. The wall I am still touching.

*Me. Meee. Meeee.*

I remove my fingers from the stone. The noise stops. I touch it again. The noise starts.

"Touch the wall, Jess. Then you'll hear it."

Jess touches the wall. "Nothing."

Shalini tries. "Me neither."

I touch the stone lower down.

*Meeeee.*

I take my hand away. The noise stops. Then there's a click and a crunch and the blocks of stone move.

**2**

*Summary:*

*Something odd is happening.*

*Plan A: Ignore it.*

I step away, bumping into Jess. The blocks of stone slide backwards and sideways with a grating noise that sets my teeth on edge.

"Uh-oh," says Shalini, as a doorway appears. "Look at the cobwebs. They're sticky cobwebs. Dangly cobwebs. Big, sticky, dangly cobwebs."

"It's a secret stairway!" says Jess. "I've always wanted a secret stairway! And you opened it." She's pointing at me.

"I did not!"

"You did, Twink," says Shalini.

"You did," says Jess. "Look." There's a strange letter carved into the stone I touched. It glows red and disappears.

Shalini whispers, "It's a rune." She whispers it dramatically like an announcement that should be followed by a deep *dum, dum, dum* of scariness.

Jess is now completely overexcited. "It has to lead to one of the abandoned towers," she squeals, grinning a wide grin of delight and eagerness. "There's bound to be a secret tower room at the top of a secret stairway! Let's find out!" She jumps into the doorway and turns back, waiting for us to join her.

Both Shalini and I answer, "No!"

Shalini pulls her back out. "There could be Toadspit Terrors in there! Look at the cobwebs!"

I shake my head and agree. "Jess. I absolutely refuse to investigate a secret staircase full of the possibility of Toadspit Terrors."

She answers with, "Shush."

I think she's copying my shush from before but then I hear what she hears. Voices. Coming along the landing above.

"Dominique and Arwen," says Shalini. Her shoulders sag.

Jess pulls my arm. "We can't let Dominique and Arwen know we've found a secret staircase," she whispers. "This is *our* secret staircase. Quick. Hide!" She pushes me through the doorway before I can say, *What art thou doing*, and drags Shalini in after us.

"This is not hiding," I whisper. A cobweb lands on my nose. I shudder and swipe it off in case there's a small beastie attached. "I think Dominique and Arwen will definitely notice the big hole in the wall that was not there yesterday."

"Then we must close the big hole in the wall," Jess whispers back. "There must be a rune on this side." She spots it. It's faint, like an old scribble that someone's tried to rub out. She presses it. Nothing happens. She presses again. Nothing happens.

"I think it has to be you, Twink," she says.

Shalini squeaks, "But if Twink closes the door we could be trapped!"

"And if Twink doesn't close the door Dominique and Arwen will tell Ms Thorn about the staircase and it won't be our secret staircase, it will be Ms Thorn's secret staircase and we'll never get to investigate it!"

She grabs my hand and pushes it against the rune before I can stop her. I hear *Mee. Meeee. Meeeeoowww.*

"It's a cat!"

"What is?" says Jess.

"The mysterious noise. I can hear a cat!"

The rune glows red and the blocks slide back into place. The last one cuts us off completely from the rest of Toadspit Towers. It's pitch black. We brighten our hat-lights and they shine down from the brims like spotlights on a stage.

"Uh-oh," says Shalini. "I would just like to state that in my opinion this is a bad idea. No good ever comes from hiding in secret stairways and closing stone doorways."

Jess lifts her chin and shines her hat on the ceiling. The cobwebs are thick but most look dusty and old, clumpy and grey. Not like the shiny white cobwebs we swept from the corridors two days ago. Not like the giant sticky cobweb of death that I encountered as I failed to escape from my destiny.

"It's scary," says Shalini nervously. She unhooks her spoon charm from her bracelet. She has three charms. So does Jess. A witchwood spoon, a cauldron and a book. My bracelet belonged to Greats-Grandma Ursula and I have the same charms as my friends plus one extra charm. The witchwood tree. The tree lives in the centre of the Toadspit Garden of Doom and it's where all the magic comes from in Toadspit Towers.

"It's just dirty," says Jess.

"I don't like dirty," says Shalini. She holds her spoon up. "Witchwood, witchwood, do the deed, change to be what I now need." Her spoon changes into a broom. She twizzles it on her finger and it swooshes the cobwebs around the broom like a stick of candy floss.

I touch the wall. It feels cold.

*Mee. Mee. Meeeowww!*

"I can still hear the cat," I say. "I think it's calling to me. I don't think it's Oddbod. A witchwood cat's meows are more flutey. This sounds like a real cat."

*Meeow. Meeeooowww. Meeeeeeooowww!*

"Maybe it's a kitten. A cute, cuddly kitten." I shine my hat-light up the steps. "I *must* go up the staircase. I *must* save the cute, cuddly kitten."

I set off.

"Come back!" shouts Shalini. "No good ever comes of following mysterious noises either, Twink. There could be disastrous consequences!"

3

**Summary:**

*I am being pulled up the tower by love.*

"But pussycat is up there," I say, not stopping. "And pussycat needs me."

I keep climbing. A web breaks across my face. I leave it there. There's a thick rope looped on the curved wall, to hang on to, but I don't need it. I feel light. As if I could float up to the top of the staircase.

"But what about the webs and the beasties?" shouts Shalini from below. "We can't just ignore the possibility of beasties!"

I drag my fingers lightly on the wall as I climb.

*Meeeeeeoooooowwwww.*

The cat-voice sounds sad. Miserable. Desperate.

20

Suddenly something knocks into my hat and I am overtaken by Shalini's broomstick twizzling overhead, sweeping away the cobwebs. Another one follows it as I hear my friends running up the steps behind me. Jess shouts, "Get those beasties, broomsticks!"

The stairs go round and round and round and I go dizzy as we climb up and up and up but I do not stop.

"Are we nearly there yet?" says Jess. She's panting.

I drag my fingers. The meowing grows louder and longer with every step until I turn a corner and there are no more. There's a small landing and a door.

It's a small door. Ms Thorn would have to bend in half to get through it but it would be the perfect height for Ms Sage, the headmistress. It isn't witchwood, it's dark red and dull. The spider's web candyfloss broomsticks are leaning against it.

Jess bumps into me. My fingers leave the wall and I can't hear the meow. I feel heavier. Normal heavy. And a little bit odd.

"Oh, a door," she says, panting. "Yay." Her

overexcitement has been dampened by lack of oxygen.

Shalini puffs her way up the last few steps and sees the door. "Uh-oh. Maybe we shouldn't open it? Maybe we should go back down and tell someone? That's definitely the safest and most sensible thing to do," she says. She looks from me to Jess and back to me. "But we're not going to do that, are we? We're going to open the door, aren't we?"

"Of course we are," says Jess. "We have to save the cat."

There's a handle on the door, the sort you get on gates with a latch. I reach for it.

"Wait!" says Shalini. "Spoons!" She pushes past me and grabs her broom. She twizzles the webs off the broom and into a corner, where they sit like a giant cocoon. Jess does the same. They change the brooms back to spoons with a "Witchwood, witchwood, be my spoon" chant.

Jess holds hers in front of her like a weapon. "Ready," she says. Shalini copies and nods to me.

I press the latch down. It's stiff, then it gives way and lifts, but the door doesn't open. I push it with my shoulder and Jess joins in. One, two, three pushes and the door gives way and the two of us stumble and fall into the room. Jess is on top of me, squashing me, and we're blinded by the sunlight pouring in from the tall windows.

"Wow!" says Jess, shading her eyes. "I was right! We're at the top of the school." She leaps off me and dashes to the nearest window. "We are! We're in the tallest tower! I can see everything!"

Now that she's got her breath back her excitement level has gone way past *overexcited* and is fast approaching *explode*. I join her. We look out over the other towers and rooftops. Then we hear Shalini gasping and whizz back round. Spoons at the ready.

Shalini is frozen in the doorway. She's doing a look from *The Book of Absolute Joy.* "Look at the BOOKS!" she shouts. "Thousands of BOOKS!"

There are stone shelves in between each window and they are packed with books and rolled-up scrolls.

Shalini takes one step in, then another, then she runs at the shelves as if she needs to hug all the books in one gigantic hug. She stops with her nose squished against the spine of a large red leather book.

The books look old with dark covers and golden lettering. There's a cabinet under each window. The first is full of empty potion bottles with faded labels written in old-fashioned handwriting. The glass doors are grimy and greasy. There's a table and chair in the middle of the room, piled high with more books.

Jess gasps and tugs on my sleeve. "Look, Twink! It's you!" She's pointing to a painting propped up on a shelf on the other side of the table. It has a golden frame of leaves and roses. It is a picture of me. My hair, my smile, my nose, but I'm wearing old-fashioned clothes. There are other paintings stacked behind this one.

"Why would there be a painting of you in a secret room?" says Shalini, leaving her books. She looks closer. "Oh. It isn't you, Twink. Look at the hat."

She's right. The hat is orange. A happy orange, velvety and warm with a wide brim. There's a tarnished brass label at the bottom of the frame. *Marietta Toadspit On Her Eleventh Birthday*.

I tilt the picture forward. The ones behind are all of Marietta too. She's a bit older in each. In the last she has a kitten on her shoulder. A ball of white fluff with blue eyes and a black button nose. Not an ac-chew-al button. The title says *Marietta and Jacobus*.

Her hat is darker now, like autumn leaves in Granny's garden. She looks annoyed. Her bracelet is full of charms. There's the usual cauldron, book and spoon, plus a rose, a bottle, a key, a broomstick, a clock, a bell, a shell and a tiny pair of knitting needles. There may be more round the other side.

"That kitten is so cute!" says Jess. She hooks her spoon back on to her bracelet. "Jacobus. Sounds like Jacopuss. I love kittens. I asked for one for my fifth birthday but Mam misheard and knit me a pair of mittens. They were really cosy though. Ooh, look at the funny little men."

There's a shelf with an army of little red clay statues. They're all identical. They have round holes for mouths. One has a tiny scroll rolled up and slotted in.

"Golems," says Shalini. "Mindless beings doomed to obey the instruction on the scroll." We look amazed at her knowledge. "Arwen did a *Toadspit Times* issue on them," she says.

"And look," Jess moves on. "Tiny Toadspit

Terrors! Tiny marble spider statues. That one looks just like Scary!" I move away.

The table is covered with wobbly piles of books of all shapes and sizes and there's a large snow globe sitting on the shortest pile. There's a dead plant inside. It's grey with a thick stem and a top that looks like an umbrella of dried flowers. There's a red rune carved into the thick witchwood base, the same rune as the one in the stones, and a name. *The Gellica Charm.* I tap the glass and the snow swirls around the plant. This is not a fun, winter-wonderland snow globe. It's dreary.

Jess joins me. She moves the globe to look at the books underneath. "Ooooh, Twink!" she says as if she's found something special. "This book is awesome! It's a journal. Guess whose." She doesn't wait for me to guess. She picks it up and shows me.

4

***Summary:***

*We have discovered a secret room and there have been no disastrous consequences.*

The cover of the book is dark-brown leather with *The Journal of Marietta Toadspit* written across the middle in gold letters. The edges of the pages are gold too.

"This is brilliant!" she says. "This is probably the best book in the whole library. I am holding in my hands *ALL* of Marietta's secrets. If you knew how to open this you could find out exactly what happened to make her go bad! You'd know why Marietta cursed her mother's ghost to stay in her Toadspit doll. You'd know why she cursed her mother to remain headmistress until another Toadspit turned up. You'd know why she left Toadspit Towers never to return. All you need is the key and you'll know EVERYTHING you need to know!"

She spots another interesting title at the bottom of another pile and hands me the journal as she says, "Oooh, now look what I've found! Useful."

It feels weird holding something that ac-chew-ally belonged to one of my ancestors. I tried to keep a diary once, which is like a journal, because actresses do that and then they publish them just before they die and tell everyone their secrets and annoy the other people in the book. But I was far too busy to fill it in. I didn't get past January.

I pull at the cover but it won't budge and the pages feel like they're stuck together with magical superglue. I put the book down and search the desk for a key but don't find it. I feel like I've been given a sticky, dribbly cherry pie full of tasty sweetness but then someone has poured gloop over it. I am suffering from disappointment.

Jess props another book up against her chest. It's huge and heavy.

"*Ruleth the Runes* by Doris Periwinkle," she says. "This will help next term when we do rune writing. I won't need to spend my ticks on a rune book," she says. "I have a free rune book!" She undoes a button on her skirt's waistband and a pocket falls open. She holds the corner of the book against it and the book is sucked inside.

I am stunned. I name that pocket *The Pocket of Usefulness*. "That is the most useful pocket ever!" I say. "How many ticks do I need for a pocket such as that?"

"None," says Jess. "You already have one. Didn't you know?"

"How could I possibly know? Didn't you hear Ms Thorn? I am *IGNORANT*! I'm new to everything." I check my skirt. I do have a button! I open it and look in. It's dark.

"It's like the cauldron. It grows to fit what's inside," says Jess. She puts another book in hers, *Potions for the Powerful*, to show me what to do. Shalini sees. She gasps a horrified gasp.

"Jess! You can't possibly take a book out of here," she says. "They need to be catalogued, recorded, ordered, arranged ... stamped! It'll be chaos without a proper library system and … it's stealing."

"I am not stealing. I'm borrowing," says Jess. "And, anyway, it belongs to Twink. Everything in this room belongs to Twink."

"Jess can have the book, Shalini," I say. "Because tech-nic-ally she's right. It is all mine."

"But this room is too important to keep to ourselves," says Shalini. "Ms Sage might not have copies of these books. These books could be unique." Her voice squeaks as she says "unique". "We have to tell her."

"Not yet," I say. *Maybe never*, I think.

"Shalini," says Jess. "Twink hasn't found the cat yet and we can't possibly tell anyone about this *Room of Wonderful Things* until she's found the cat."

*That's a good name for it*, I think. *I will adopt it.*

"And," continues Jess, "I would just like to remind you that we are only here in this room now because we followed the mysterious cat-voice and climbed the secret staircase to the secret room *and* this has not led to disastrous consequences."

"Not yet," says Shalini, and she turns away to straighten the books on the nearest shelf.

I suddenly realise I haven't thought about the cat since I fell into the room, which is odd because my head had been so full of the cat-voice that nothing else had mattered. I touch the nearest stone shelf. I hear a tiny, sharp *meeoow* as if the cat is cross and I am immediately overwhelmed with guilt.

"Poor pussycat," I say.

"Did you hear it?" says Jess.

"I did." I feel light again. Floaty.

"So, where is it?" she says, looking around. "Puss, puss, puss. Meow. Meow. Meow."

I ignore her and slide my fingers along the shelf. *Meow.*

"*Must* find pussycat." I slide them the other way.

*Meeoow.*

"*Must* go this way."

*Meeeoooow. Meeeeooooow. Meeeeeooooooow!*

"Pussycat *needs* me. Pussycat *must* have me. Pussycat *loves* me. Pussycat! I will *find* you! I will *save* you! I *feel* you!"

Shalini is now close behind me. Jess is in front.

"Why are you speaking like that?" whispers Shalini. "Jess, why is she speaking like that?"

I follow the sound across the shelves, under the windows and the meowing gets louder and louder.

"Pussycat, pussycat, where are you now?" I'm purring. "*Purrrrrrrrrrrr.*"

*Meeeeeeeeeooooooooooow!*

"Jess!" says Shalini. "Why is she purring?"

"I don't know," says Jess. "It's all a bit weird. Twink, stop purring. You're freaking me out."

"*Purrrrrrrrrrrrr*. Pussycat is here. *Purrrrrrr.*"

"Where?" says Jess.

I'm between a pair of windows. In front of a set of stone shelves crammed with books and ornaments.

The shelf at nose height looks like the mantelpiece in Granny's kitchen, where she keeps her collection of "magical oddities".

There's a teapot with two handles and two spouts, a silver spoon, a Jack-in-the-Box with an evil-looking Jack wobbling backwards and forwards, a large iron key, a pair of red boots worn down at the heel, and a blue and white bowl with words painted around the edge. *Wash me, wish me, clean and true, so I may be of help to you.*

"Nobody touch anything," says Shalini.

"I wasn't going to," says Jess.

The sunshine is shining through an amber bottle

making the back of the shelf golden and warm. Leaning against the wall there's a horn with a silver rim and a crystal kitten that would fit perfectly on my palm.

*Meeeeeeeooooooooowww!*

"It's a crystal pussycat," I say, with a big sigh. "*Purrrrrrrr*. I've found him."

Jess and Shalini are both leaning over my shoulders. Jess is pressing down with her chin.

"Uh-oh," she says loudly in my ear. "That isn't just a crystal pussycat. There's a silver creature charm inside. It's Jacopuss!"

**5**

**Summary:**

*We have found Marietta's cat! I love Marietta's cat.*

It *is* Jacobus. There's a silver kitten-shaped creature charm buried in the middle of the crystal kitten.

"Why would someone trap a creature charm in crystal?" says Shalini. "Whatever you do, don't touch it until we know the answer." She carefully moves the other artefacts left and right with her spoon until we can see the kitten properly.

*Meeeeeooooowwww*

"Poor pussycat. *Purrrrrrrrrrr.*" I can't stop myself. I pick it up.

"Put it down, Twink!" squeaks Shalini. "We don't know if it's safe and I think it probably isn't."

There's a flash of blue in the charm's silver eyes. He stares at me through the crystal.

"Uh-oh," says Jess. "Look at the eyes!"

I feel floaty but my hat feels heavy. Like it's trying to push a thought into my head. I think the thought is – Danger. I ignore it.

*Meeeeeoooooow! Mistress Marietta, I be sorry! Free me and I'll be good. I promise thee.*

"Pussycat is speaking to me!" I sigh because he thinks I am Marietta. How wonderful. "Don't be sorry, pussycat. I will free you."

*You know it was not my fault. You know I always get the blame because the witchwood cats hate me! You must make your mother forgive and forget.*

I gasp in horror. "The cats hate my pussycat! Bad witchwood cats. Naughty witchwood cats!"

"Oh, that can't be good," says Jess. She pushes me towards the table.

"Don't drop him, Twink," says Shalini. "The crystal could shatter."

"Give the kitten to me," says Jess, as if she's in

charge of me. "It's making you weird."

I don't want to do that so I hiss at her.

Suddenly she grabs Jacobus by his crystal head! I pull. She pulls.

"Let go!" she shouts. "There's something wrong with you!"

"You let go!" I shout. "He's mine!"

She drags Jacobus out of my hands but he slips through her fingers and flies up above my head. Too high to catch.

Jess falls backwards into the table. The books topple, the table topples and the snow globe is flipped up next to Jacobus. I jump up to grab him but the snow globe is in the way. I bash it aside. My fingers catch on the rune sticking out from the wooden base, and it moves. There's a loud click as the globe falls to the floor and Jacobus the crystal kitten drops into my hands, yowling with laughter.

He doesn't sound like a cute, cuddly kitten now. He sounds like a tomcat! My hat twitches. I hear the thought again – DANGER! This time, I listen. My

head clears. I cease to be floaty. I am LIVING IN
THE LAND OF APPALLED AND SHOCKED!

"He was using persuasion on me!" I announce. I
hold the crystal kitten as far away from me as I can.

"We guessed," says Jess.

"Don't drop him!" says Shalini.

*Thou art in trouble now, Mistress,* says Jacobus.
*This is worse than when I cast the pimple pox,
and the knee-twizzler, and the blight, but this time
it definitely isn't my fault! It's all yours! Thou hast
opened the Snow Globe Of Gellica!*

Oh dungpats! That doesn't sound good.

The snow globe is on the floor. The rune on the
base has split in half and changed from red to black.
The glass is glistening, sparkling and dissolving then
suddenly we are surrounded by freezing, stinging,
flakes of snow and swirling, whirling, needles of ice!
The wind whips the pages of the books, stirring up
the dust and cobwebs. We are in the middle of an ac-
chew-al snow tornado!

Jacobus yowls with glee then bursts into song.

*Here we go round the gellica tree, the gellica tree, the gellica tree! Here we go round the gellica tree on a cold and frosty morning! We spin the gellica out of the school, out of the school, out of the school. We spin the gellica out of the school on a cold and frosty morning!*

The dead plant grows roots, stem and flowers. Changing from deathly grey to the palest purple. It spins faster and faster.

Jacobus keeps singing. My clothes are dragged around me and suddenly I'm spinning on the spot. We're all spinning on the spot! The books fly up and they're spinning too. Jess is dodging them. Shalini looks like she's juggling them.

I'm gripping the crystal kitten of catastrophe by the neck and I want to drop him but I daren't drop him. What if Shalini's right? What if I drop him and the crystal shatters and I release Jacobus the monster of persuasiveness into Toadspit Towers? A monster who curses people with the pimple-pox and the knee-twizzler? They do not sound pleasant. And what was the blight he released? Granny's nettles had blight once and she had to burn them all. A blight is not a good thing.

Jacobus meows. His blue eyes flash, lighting up his crystal prison. *Oh, Marietta! What will your mother do when she finds out you've broken the Gellica Charm and DOOMED THE SCHOOL!*

Dungpats! I fear dooming the school will definitely come under magical mayhem and if Ms Thorn ever finds out she'll make me eat gloop forever. If we ever escape the *Room of Disaster.*

**6**

**Summary:**

*I have more questions:*

*Does Jacobus really think I'm Marietta?*

*Does he think Greats-Grandma Ursula is still alive?*

*What's a Gellica Charm and have I ac-chew-ally doomed the school? AND How will we get out of this?*

"Twink! Jess! Hold hands," shouts Shalini. "I have an idea." She reaches out to grab Jess but misses and they twirl away from me.

I can't hold hands. I'm holding Jacobus. Then I have an idea of my own too but I have absolutely no idea if my idea is a good idea. There is always the possibility that my idea may lead to even more disastrous consequences.

My idea is this: I must drop Jacobus into the only safe place I can think of. The only place he won't be shattered by flying books and artefacts. My Pocket of Usefulness.

This is not easy to accomplish because I am spinning like a ballerina and my skirt is tangled around my bottom and the front is at the back, then the back is at the back, then the back is at the front and my tie is twisting round my neck and spiralling upwards like a noose.

I do it and, oh joy, I can't hear his annoying tomcat yowling any more.

Shalini and Jess grab hands. They reach out to me. "Hold hands, Twink," shouts Shalini again. I reach out and they grab me, jerking me to a stop. Then we start spinning together around the plant that is now as tall as a hollyhock. We rise from the floor. It's like a super-fast game of the hokey-cokey. Left legs in. Left legs out. Both legs in. Both legs out. Both legs up and turning all about.

"Uh-oh. Look at the walls," shouts Shalini. "What's

happening to the walls!" The walls are oozing tiny drops of pinky-purple glittery liquid.

"What is it?" I yell.

"How would I know?" she yells back. "I've only been at witch school for six weeks! I don't know everything!"

"Don't look at me," yells Jess. "I have no answers."

The drops are being sucked out of the wall by the tornado. They're whizzing around our heads. I hold my breath in case I breathe one in. They spin past us, to the plant. They sink into the grey stem like pinky-purple spots.

"Hold my skirt!" cries Shalini. "And hang on tight!" She lets go of our hands and we grab her skirt. She holds her spoon above her head and shouts, "Witchwood, witchwood, hear me plead, change to be what I now need." Her spoon changes back into a broomstick and she cries, "ZOOM BROOM! Out of the room!"

The broom zooms up dragging Shalini, Jess and me with it. We fly across the ceiling, down the wall

and out of the open door.

It drops us on the landing. Jess and I pull the door shut and then we fall on Shalini with a joint hug of hugeness and tightness.

"Shalini, you are an amazing witch," I gasp.

"You are the BEST," says Jess.

She pushes us both off, folds her arms and glares at us. She is not good at glares. In fact, she is terrible at glares. Her hat is trembling.

"I *told* you both it was a bad idea. I *told* you both we should tell. I *told* you both nothing good *EVER* comes from a secret tower room up a secret staircase and that following mysterious cat voices would lead to disastrous consequences!"

Jess and I look sheepish. This involves looking sideways at each other without moving our heads. Jess puts her hands behind her back. I fiddle with my skirt, twisting it back into place. Wondering if she has finished. She hasn't.

"And now we've got a massive problem. We've unlocked something. Unleashed something. And we don't even know what it is! And what's that leaking out of the walls? What if it's important? It probably *IS* important!"

She might be finished now.

"And what about the cat," she says. "A cat who is now flying round in the chaos and the mayhem. A cat who will probably crash into something and the crystal will shatter and it'll be free, and who knows what that will mean for the school, and we'll have two problems we can't solve and not one." She's running out of breath.

"Ah," I say, thinking she ac-chew-ally has finished. "You don't need to worry about the cat. He isn't in the *Room of Disaster*. He's in my pocket."

Shalini's terrible glare is replaced with a look from *The Book of – What!!!* This is a look that suits her because she has such big eyes anyway.

I reach into my Pocket of Usefulness and I immediately hear him again but my hat tingles and I resist the pull of persuasiveness.

*Mistress! Let me out! Why hast thou trapped me in the dark! Mistress Marietta!*

"He wants to get out."

"Don't let him." Shalini grabs my wrist. "This could be a good thing. As long as he's in your pocket he isn't a problem, is he? He can't escape, can he?"

She asks Jess not me because I am obviously not an expert on pockets of usefulness having only just discovered their existence.

"I don't think so," says Jess.

"Good," I say. "Then he can stay in there and I can forget all about him until we have a plan to put everything right again. A plan that does not involve telling Ms Thorn I have broken the Gellica Charm and doomed the school."

"What?!" say my friends together.

"That's what Jacobus said, but he was probably lying. Exaggerating, maybe."

I'm not sure they believe that. I'm not sure I believe that.

"Did he say how you've doomed the school?" says Jess.

"Will it fall down?" says Shalini. She's looking up for cracks.

"I have no idea. He just said doomed. Let's discuss it over tea," I say, as if I am looking forward to gloop. I set off down the stairs. They pester me to tell them every little thing Jacobus said as they follow me down.

Shalini keeps up with the questions and the worries

and the advice to *Tell Ms Sage Everything!* all the way to the bottom of the stairs. I touch the rune and cross my fingers that it will open.

The stones slide and we peep along the corridor. It's empty. We step out and I close the doorway. The rune disappears and there is no sign it ever existed.

"There we are, Shalini," I say. "Everything's back to normal. No one would ever suspect there is a secret staircase behind that wall. I bet no one knows the *Room of Disaster* exists and no one knows I have a three-hundred-year-old creature in my pocket. So no one is going to find out about Storm Mayhem. We have plenty of time to fix this. Years, maybe."

"Months?" says Jess.

"Years? Months? More like days. Maybe even hours," says Shalini. "But what if—"

She stops talking. She's looking behind me.

I turn around.

"You are late," says Dominique.

"And you are behaving suspiciously," says Arwen.

We step away from the wall as if we're not interested in it. We do a look from *The Book of Innocence.*

"Suspicion always haunts the guilty mind, Arwen," I say. "What have *you* been up to?"

"Ms Thorn has sent I to fetch you," says Dominique. "You are to be fined one tick for every five minutes of lateness. So far you have been fined three ticks. Each."

Oh great, now I don't have zero ticks. I have less than zero ticks.

Arwen says, "Ms Sage says Wrinkle must come to tea. That tea cannot begin until the *Saviour of the*

*School* arrives." She does *Saviour of the School* in air quotes.

"We were just coming," says Jess. "And it's *Twinkle* not Wrinkle."

"Twinkle," says Dominique – she says it like this – Twin-Kal, with the emphasis on the K. "Twinkle should comply and conform with Ms Sage's instructions and not waste time." She looks me up and down as if she's only just noticed me properly. "You are dishevelled. Your hair is a mess." She inspects Shalini and Jess too. Our shirts are half-tucked, our ties are loose, our tights are wrinkly.

Dominique tsks. *Tsk.* "You have not tidied yourselves. You are being disrespectful to the memory of Ms Ursula Toadspit. You are Toadspit witches and Toadspit witches must be tidy and trim at all times. You know this."

She is, of course, tidy and trim with each tight black curl carefully tweaked into place under her smooth red hat, her cat-tie tied with a knot of neatness and her shirt tucked in all the way round. She is a perfect

example of tidiness. Arwen is almost perfectly tidy but strands of wavy red hair are escaping her plaits. She's a red hat too. They're both fifth generation witches, the same as Ms Thorn.

Normally, unreasonable demands and criticisms from Dominique would trigger a moment of annoyance and a refusal to comply resulting in a hands-on-hips moment of defiance, but I have more to think about than Dominique and Arwen's bossiness, so I act chirpy and agree to their demands.

"Dominique and Arwen, fairest of girls, sometimes Best and Brightest of Toadspit Towers, thou art just the messengers and do not deserve my anger. Lead on and I shall comply with Ms Sage and Ms Thorn's desires."

I don't wait. I set off. I get to the dining hall first.

The witchwood roots around the door are smooth and warm to the touch. I place my hand in the centre of a Celtic pattern, the root-knot unwinds and transforms into a hand. I'm getting used to this. We do a slow high-five and I'm filled with happy fizzingling as my thumb connects and I say, "I give thanks to the witchwood." My witchwood thumb sends little bursts of joy through my body.

I am doing a happy dance inside and suddenly I have an idea of genius. Maybe the witchwood can fix the Gellica Charm? Maybe the witchwood remembers Jacobus!

I keep my connection to the roots and put my other hand in my pocket.

*Oh, the dark! The gloom! The terrible gloom!*

A fizzingle fizzes from the roots, through my thumb, my hand, my body, and into my other hand. It reaches the pocket and *POW!* It changes into a *HUGE BUZZINGLE* that throws me back, off the witchwood!

*Meeeeeooooooowwwll,* cries Jacobus. *The tree! Why art thou torturing me with the tree, Mistress!*

I pull my hand out of my pocket. I must be doing a look from *The Book of – What?* now because both Shalini and Jess say it.

"What?"

I do not answer because Dominique is behind Jess. "You are taking too long," she says. "And you are obviously bothering the witchwood." She struts past me then stops. "You are dawdling and delaying to be annoying. You are not complying. You must comply." She continues her strut.

I am annoyed. Now instead of an *Answer* I have another *Question*.

*Why did the witchwood buzzingle Jacobus?*

I have no answer.

The dining hall is dark because the sun is setting. It looks quite pretty with all the hat-lights shining down on the girls. The seven achievement Boards of Embarrassment that hang on the walls have altered since lunchtime. They have been updated with ticks earned and lost.

Images of Shalini and Jess are still in the smaller Best and Brightest golden board, having replaced Dominique who had been Best and Brightest for most of the year. They are joint winners because they earned so many ticks trying to save me as I failed to

escape my destiny.

Dominique's name is at the top of the red board, Arwen's at the bottom. I am the only name on the seventh board, the white board, so I am both top and bottom. I have minus four. Four! I should have run faster. The comment still says Unknown Potential with the addition, in brackets, of Saviour of the School.

I look behind me at the wall of witchwood dolls, *The Witches of Toadspit Towers* display. I wonder if Marietta's doll is up there, not just Greats-Grandma Ursula's. I'd like to go and check but Dominique is glaring at me to hurry up.

The witchwood cats are sleeping in the roots growing around the doors and edges of the room. There are no kittens ready to snap their tails from the roots but I see two curled up, growing like flower buds. There's no sign of Oddbod.

"Look out," says Jess. A creature whizzes past my ankles, making me jump. It's like a ferret crossed with a badger. It streaks across the room towards the teachers' table. I name it a Badget. It has a small scroll in its mouth. It jumps up, drops it on to a bigger scroll draped over the table and scoots away again as Ms Thorn unrolls it.

Ms Thorn normally has a blood-red, smooth and silky hat but today it's a little bit creased at the top as if she's been thinking a lot and struggling to teach an *ignorant* person. She's wearing a red fitted suit with a high collar that's holding her chin up. She looks – official. Her creature, Fangus the bat, is hanging from her ear, nibbling on something juicy.

Ms Thorn taps the smaller scroll with her pointy red fingernails and the other three teachers bend forward. I call them Ms Floppy-Orange, Ms Puckered-Purple and Ms Crumpled-Crimson after their hats because I can't remember their names. They are all very old. Older than Granny. Maybe old enough to be Granny's mum, or even Granny's granny.

Ms Sage is also there. Her hat, a golden-yellow mix of muddled-up textures, is rippling, which is a new development. Her dress is what Granny Wart would call fancy-frippery. Swirls of yellow and golden velvet, lace and silk that go in and out with her chubby bits. It stops below her knees, just above the ears on her pink bunny slippers.

She notices our arrival and she smiles her smiley smile of persuasion at the three of us then says something we can't hear. I suspect, "You must sit down, dears," because we speed up and sit down. The table is already set for five.

Ms Sage's persuasiveness doesn't feel the same as Jacobus's persuasiveness. This feels like sensible persuasiveness as if she's just giving me a little push to do something I was going to do anyway.

There's a whoosh over my head and another scroll

is delivered. This time it's Horatio, Ms Sage's tiny owl. She takes the scroll and whispers something in his ear. He spins from a live owl into a silver charm on her bracelet.

"What is going on at the teachers' table?" whispers Jess.

"I have no idea and I do not need another question I have no answer to," I whisper back.

Ms Sage draws a mark on the small scroll and another on the big scroll. The words fly off the small one on to the big one just as the doors from the kitchen bang open and Ms Brewbody leads a row of floating trays into the dining hall.

There's a hooray from some of the girls. I notice that not all of them are as tidy and trim as they were when I arrived two days ago but I don't think I should be blamed for this. There is such a thing as personal responsibility.

A tray stops at our table and the plates float off. Dominique has a slice of hot crusty bread and a bowl of macaroni cheese with the cheese all bubbly on top. Arwen has the same, minus the bread.

The smell of the bread makes me think of Granny's home-made bloomers with their crusts sprinkled with crushed nuts and seeds. I close my eyes and imagine her cutting thick brown slices, toasting them by the fire until they are crisp on the outside and warm and fluffy on the inside, spreading the melting butter from corner to corner, imagine us curling up in the cosy chairs with cups of tea to wash it down ... then there's a clunk as a bowl lands in front of me, forcing me to face reality. I open my eyes.

I do not have hot crusty bread. I have GLOOP. Because, as previously mentioned, I have fewer than NO ticks and I have earned NO food.

This gloop looks even more disgusting than breakfast gloop and dinner gloop. Thicker. Greyer. Gloopier. I suspect if I leave it to go cold, which I intend to do, it will turn into a brick.

"Have some potato," says Jess, passing me half of her baked potato without waiting for an answer.

"And a sausage," says Shalini, passing it over.

Before I can object to their generosity Arwen says, in a voice of concern, "How does it make you feel, Tinkle? Having to rely on charity because you've earned fewer than no ticks?"

She sucks up a forkful of macaroni cheese as if it's the best food anyone has ever eaten. I call this gloat-eating. It must be done slowly and with a look of pure enjoyment. Although, I think she's just discovered it's a bit too hot and she's trying not to let on. Which serves her right.

Jess explains slowly. "This is *sharing*, Arwen. This is what GOOD witches do," she says. She nods her nod of wiseness and offers me a spoonful of peas. I decline them. Not because of Arwen. I don't like peas.

Shalini joins in. She's been much braver with Dominique and Arwen since she faced Vernon, the vicious veraptor, and won. "I'd be happy to share my other sausage with you too, Arwen."

Dominique answers for her. "Arwen has no need to accept food from others. Arwen has conformed and complied. Arwen has earned enough ticks to feed herself." She looks at me as if I'm supposed to finish the sentence with *unlike Twinkle.*

I smile. She doesn't. I take a bite of sausage. It tastes good. I smile again. She doesn't. She looks away. I win. Something bumps the back of my legs. It's Oddbod. He meows a flutey witchwood cat meow of greeting and jumps up on to my knee. He has a letter in his mouth. He drops it as I scratch behind his

odd-sized ears, the big one first, then the small. He's sniffing my pocket.

Jess picks up the letter and turns it over. She reads the address silently, not showing us, then she holds it up and looks over the top.

"Oooh! A letter. But who is it for?" she says. "Dominique? Arwen? Shalini? Me? Twinkle?" She pauses. "No. None of those. It's for…" She waits. She waits some more. She flips it round. "Daisy Wart! Maybe it's fan mail, Twink? Maybe you're famous!"

She passes it over. I have decided to keep my original name, Daisy Wart, as my stage name because, well … Twinkle Toadspit? How would that look on the posters? *The Tempest* with Twinkle Toadspit. *Much Ado About Nothing* starring Twinkle Toadspit. Or Twinkle Toadspit in *All's Well That Ends Well*. Lots of actors have two names.

"Open it, Twink," says Shalini. "Maybe Jess is right. It could be fan mail. Maybe someone loved your Bottom."

Arwen sniggers. "Or hated her Bottom."

I see Dominique looking but not looking. I'm not sure I want to open it while they are there. What if it's a bad review? But who would send me a bad review?

"I am opening it," I say. "Look, this is me opening it." I rip the envelope open and unfold a letter. It isn't fan mail. "It's from Mr Marlow."

"Read it out," says Jess.

I comply. I read it loud enough for Dominique and Arwen to hear because I have read the first few words to myself and they are GOOD WORDS!

**Summary:**

*I am an ac-chew-al actwitch! My career is NOT OVER!*

*"Dear Daisy, Well done for an excellent performance last night. The reviews are in and the response has been amazing! Your magnificent Bottom was noticed by the leading light of the local amateur-dramatics society, the legendary Ms Dench, and she has approached me with an exciting proposition!"*

I pause for dramatic effect. Dominique is actively ignoring me. I continue.

*"She has invited the pupils of St Bluebottle's drama group on tour! She wants to show* A Midsummer Night's Dream *far and wide, well, far and wide*

*within the local area anyway! It's a great chance to exhibit your Bottom to a much bigger audience!"*

I pause again. My heart is soaring! I am living in the land of SUCCESS! My career is NOT OVER! All thoughts of dealing with the monster cat-creature in my pocket disappear. All worries about the Gellica Charm dooming the school fade away. I am an actress. Not a problem solver. I continue.

*"The tour will begin in two weeks' time and we will give ten performances in ten schools in one week."* I stop reading. "Ten performances!" I quickly do the sum. "Ten schools with approximately three hundred pupils each makes ... an audience of thirty thousand!"

Shalini whispers, "I think it's three thousand."

Dungpats. But that's still a big audience even though they won't all be watching at the same time. I continue reading.

*"And, this is the most exciting news, we will finish the tour one week later with a performance at THE THEATRE ROYAL!"*

I am living in the LAND OF DREAMS COME

TRUE!

"*As you are no longer a pupil at St Bluebottle's you will need to have your new headteacher fill in the permission slip below and return it to me by three-thirty pm tomorrow. If you are unable to appear then I need to audition for your part and I know Deirdre Kempe is very keen to reveal her Bottom.*"

Deirdre Kempe! There is no way I can let Deirdre Kempe take over my Bottom!

"Ms Sage will never allow this," says Dominique, who can't *not* tell me what to do. "You must focus on the school and forget your past life. You are a Toadspit witch. Nothing else is required of you." She folds her arms as if she has spoken the truth and so shall it be.

"Dominique's right," says Arwen. "Your acting career is finished. Over. Ended. Accept it."

"Rubbish," says Jess. "People can do two things at once." She rubs her tummy and pats her head. "See."

I say nothing. What if they are right? What if Ms Sage won't allow it? That would be a tragedy of

Shakespearean proportions! My heart sinks into a pit of despair that's quickly filling up with mud. My hat feels heavy.

"You don't know till you ask," says Shalini, nudging me.

Jess takes the letter back. "Maybe you can *make* her sign it? Now that you're *All Powerful*?" She pretends to be Ms Sage with her smile of persuasion. "You *muuuust* sign the letter. You *muuuust* let me leave witch schooooool."

"That is not allowed," says Dominique.

"We would tell," says Arwen. She flicks her plaits over her shoulders as if she's in charge of telling.

As I eat the rest of my sausage I concentrate on watching Ms Sage and the teachers. Can I ac-chew-ally use persuasion on the headmistress? Perhaps this is one of my seventh of seven superpowers!

Another creature, I name it a rabicat, delivers a scroll as I contemplate the development of *Plan A: The Make Sure Ms Sage Signs The Very Important Letter Plan*. I rehearse and visualise my performance as I eat my baked potato in silence.

Ms Sage stands up. She's leaving!

This is my moment! I leap up and start to dash across but then I remember that dashing is not in the plan. The plan is to walk a *Walk of Confidence*. I slow down. I fix my eyes on Ms Sage. I stroll to her table.

She notices. She waits. So does Ms Thorn and the other teachers. I speak to all of them with the *Voice of Certainty*. I stand tall with my hands behind my back and my chin up.

"Good morrow, Ms Sage, Ms Thorn, teachers." I smile and nod at them all. "I see the witchwood tree is bright today in the Garden of Doom and all is well in the world of Toadspit Towers."

Ms Thorn is looking at me suspiciously. Ms Sage is looking at me as if I am amusing. I focus on her and ignore Ms Thorn. I hold out my *Very Important Letter*.

"Esteemed headmistress, Ms Sage, I have a document that requires your signature."

I hand Ms Sage my letter. Folded so that the permission slip is at the top and the rest is hidden.

"Mr Marlow, who you met last night at my performance, requires your signature regarding my appearance in *A Midsummer Night's Dream*." This is tech-nic-ally not a lie. "You *must* write Ms Sage there." I transform my spoon into a pencilspoon and put a cross where she needs to sign. "And you *must* return the document to him forthwith." I say this with a smile of persuasiveness and then say, "Thank you very much," as if she's already obeyed me. She hasn't. I keep the smile on my face.

Ms Sage catches my hand and pats it. "How interesting, my dear. However I never sign anything without reading it and at the moment I am about to take to the stage to make an announcement so I'm afraid your letter will need to wait."

What? No! I continue to act confidently. "Ms Sage, my letter is *very important* and you *muuuust* sign it," I say. Maybe I need more practice at the smile of persuasiveness because it really does not seem to be working. I make the smile bigger.

"Of course, it's important to you, my dear," she says, beaming at me as if I am the most hilarious thing she's ever encountered. "But it will have to wait until I have made my own *very important announcement*."

9

**Summary:**

*Plan A: The Make Sure Ms Sage Signs The Very Important Letter Plan has had a temporary setback.*

"You really *must* reclaim your seat," says Ms Sage, when she realises I am not moving.

Now *she's* doing smiley persuasion on *me*. I consider not being persuaded. I consider arguing. I consider civil disobedience. And while I am considering all of this I walk back to my seat.

Ms Sage climbs the steps to the stage. Ms Thorn follows. The girls shush as soon as Ms Sage says, "Good afternoon, girls."

They reply, "Good afternoon, Headmistress." I don't. I am sulking. I am confused. If I'm Twinkle

Toadspit, if I'm seventh of seven, if I'm the most powerful witch in the school, how can I be so easily persuaded and WHY CAN'T I DO THE PERSUADING?

I decide to punish Ms Sage by not listening to her. But not listening is hard when only one person is talking. It's much easier not listening when a crowd is talking. A person can switch off into their own world when a crowd is talking. So even though I am actively not listening, I hear her words. She's excited. She's being quite dramatic. There's arm waving and hand gestures.

"Girls! We live in INTERESTING TIMES! Our school is FREE of the Toadspit curse laid upon it by our founder Ursula Toadspit's daughter, Marietta Toadspit."

I am now reluctantly wondering what her *very important announcement* is about. I am hoping it is not about me.

"We are finally able to become the BIGGEST, BEST and BRIGHTEST witch school in the world.

And this is all because of Ms Toadspit's heir, our wonderful Saviour of the School, Twinkle Toadspit!"

Oh dungpats, it is about me.

She claps towards me. There's polite applause from the girls. The applause fades away even though Jess tries to keep it going longer. She is last to stop. Dominique and Arwen do not stop because they did not begin.

"But, what a responsibility that is," says Ms Sage. "What a burden to lay on such a young witch, no matter how powerful. Here she is, new to witchcraft, new to the school, completely unprepared, completely untrained …"

Ms Thorn bends down and says something. Ms Sage nods.

"… and quite ignorant of our magical ways."

I cannot believe Ms Thorn has told Ms Sage to use the *I* word in front of the whole school!

"To ask Twinkle, as heir to the school, to take on the tasks of making new rules, repairing the school, and developing a new innovative curriculum on her own would be cruel and demanding," she says.

This part is true. I have absolutely no plans to do any of that.

"So. Ms Thorn, your teachers and their creatures have come up with a plan to assist her."

She steps back and Ms Thorn steps forward. She holds out the big scroll. She holds the top two corners and drops the rest. It unrolls down past her witchwood leg, on to the stage and off the edge.

"This," says Ms Thorn in a voice of firmness, "is the plan."

The scroll curls over at the top and I see the upside-down title. It's in **BOLD**. I read it as she says it. **"Our Seven Year Plan for the Development of Twinkle Toadspit."**

Seven Year Plan!!! Seven Years!!! I am living in a world of NOOOOOOOO! It has my name on it but that is NOT MY PLAN!

"There are seven stages," says Ms Thorn. "Year One. Task One. Twinkle Toadspit, the *Saviour of the School*," she sounds like she's doing Saviour of

the School in air quotes, like Arwen, "must be trained to undertake a survey of the whole school, Toadspit Towers, before a full plan of action can be agreed. The suggestions below have no particular order until said survey has been executed whereupon a more precise plan for the training of Twinkle Toadspit, the *Saviour of the School*, shall be confirmed and put into action." She pauses for breath.

She has failed to notice that I am tumbling into an abyss of annoyance. Or she's ignoring it.

"The Building: The survey will begin in the North Wing, currently inhabited by the community of pupils, teachers and creatures of Toadspit Towers. Walls, windows, floors, roofs, rafters, doors, door knockers, door hinges ..."

My life is about to become a pile of dungpats! A hill of dungpats! A mountain of dungpats! My life is going to be a life of drudgery. A life of servitude and obedience! With NO acting! NO performing! NO Oscar!

"... toilets, taps, sinks, plugs and pipes and U-bends shall be inspected and categorised on a scale of one to ten. One being in good repair and ten being in bad."

I do not believe this! I'm an actress! Not a plumber! I leap up. This is definitely a moment of determination. A hands-on-hips moment. With added foot stamp.

"HALT!" I cry. "DESIST! That plan is not my plan! That plan has not been planned by me and I

absolutely refuse to accept that plan. THIS is my plan!" I wave the *Very Important Letter* in the air. "I am going to TOUR MY BOTTOM!"

10

There's a nanosecond of silence then the hall erupts with laughter. I turn around. Jess and Shalini are trying not to laugh. Dominique is sneering. Arwen is copying.

"How perfectly dramatic, Twinkle dear," says Ms Sage, all kindness and concern. "Your performances are always so entertaining. But have you forgotten something? We had a deal."

She unhooks a nugget of gold off her bracelet. She drops it. It lands near her feet. It spins and sparkles. A hologram appears above it. It's me. I speak.

"I, Twinkle Toadspit, do solemnly declare that I will save Toadspit Towers School for Witches if I am allowed to perform my Bottom in *A Midsummer Night's Dream*." The hologram of me puts its hands

on its hips and says, "It's a deal." Then it disappears. Horatio spins from Ms Sage's bracelet and swoops down with an owly hoot. He picks up the golden nugget in his claws. He drops it into Ms Sage's hand and settles on her head, squashing her hat.

Ms Sage hooks the nugget back on to her bracelet as she says, "You performed your Bottom last night and I must say it was truly delightful. So now you must save the school, my dear. This is a binding magical agreement and cannot be broken." She nods at Ms Thorn, who continues to read the plan.

"Twinkle Toadspit will be trained in the transformation techniques required to repair and reconstruct the fabric of the school, and will eventually replace Ms Brambury, Ms Lovage and Ms Rowanstall," she nods to the ancient teachers at the table, "as Head of Maintenance. As such she will..."

I cease listening. I am experiencing severe slumping. My shoulders droop. My head droops. My arms fall by my sides. I did make that deal. Why did I make that deal? Why didn't I make a deal that meant I could do what I wanted when I wanted?! I am doomed. I will probably never perform again. My hat feels heavy with DISAPPOINTMENT. The flagstones at my feet go dull. My hat is casting a shadow instead of rainbow light. The shadow goes darker. I glance at Jess and Shalini. I suspect I'm doing a look from *The Book of Help Me*!

Jess is whispering something. She whispers it louder.

"You didn't say how many times you were allowed to perform your Bottom."

"I didn't?" I whisper back. My hat brightens. "I didn't!" Jess is a genius. My hat feels lighter as hope replaces despair. This is a moment of success! I face Ms Sage and interrupt Ms Thorn.

"Ms Sage. I declare, you are completely correct. I did indeed make that deal. BUT. I did not say, *I agree to perform my Bottom once and only once.*"

Ms Sage has lost some of the amusement from her smile.

I continue. "And as we did not agree how many times I would perform my Bottom ..." I change my position, fold my arms firmly across my chest. "... I *must* be allowed to tour as many times as I wish. As you said, the deal is binding."

Ms Sage says nothing. She's thinking quickly.

I guess this because her hat is rippling faster than before. Ms Thorn bends down and whispers something to her. I think I hear "ignorance" yet again. The woman is obsessed with the word! Ms Sage looks up and whispers something back. They mumble at each other. Ms Sage shakes her head and Ms Thorn rolls up the plan. She is doing her look of emotional blankness but a tiny patch of hat crinkles then smooths. I suspect annoyance.

"You are correct, Twinkle dear," says Ms Sage. "Our agreement did not specify the number of times you were to perform your Bottom."

I am smiling the smile of success!

"However, it also did not specify *when* you would be allowed to perform your Bottom and I rather think that decision is down to me."

Oh dungpats. My smile of success is replaced with a frown of disappointment.

"Ms Thorn has also raised an important concern regarding your magical abilities that I must take into consideration," says Ms Sage. She nods to Ms Thorn.

"Constance."

Ms Thorn speaks. She directs her words at me. "Sending a powerful, yet ignorant, witch into the normal world could result in magical mayhem and catastrophic consequences," she says. Then she steps back.

Ms Sage holds out her hand. "May I see the letter," she says. I hand it over. "Interesting," she says, reading it through thoroughly. "It's to be signed today but you will not actually tour for another two weeks."

She looks over the top of her glasses at me. I act calm. I continue to act calm. My calmness is impressive. Ms Sage suddenly smiles an exceedingly friendly smile.

"I have made up my mind. I shall allow you to perform on the dates mentioned in the letter. BUT!" She holds her hand up to stop my excitement bubbling over. "Between now and then Ms Thorn will undertake the first stage of your training and you must agree to conform and comply with her methods."

"I agree."

"Also, you must not do anything to disrupt the school, endanger the school, or interfere with the smooth running of the school before we release you to Mr Marlow."

"I agree!"

"And a Toadspit teacher shall accompany you to each performance."

"I agree!" I say.

"Then it's a deal," she says. She unhooks the golden nugget again and I record my promise but as I say, "I will not do anything to disrupt the school, endanger the school, or interfere with the smooth running of the school," I see Ms Thorn's hat-light shining on the wall behind her. The stones are glistening with dampness. It's a pinky-purple dampness.

Uh-oh.

I think I may have already broken the deal I am currently dealing.

**11**

*Summary:*

*Ms Sage has signed the letter and it is now in her pocket of usefulness ready for posting but this deal is an ac-chew-al disaster! I feel I am starring in my very own play,* The Tragedy of Twinkle Toadspit! *and I do not know my lines, or the plot. Creative improvisation may be required.*

Jess claps me on the back and Shalini shakes my hand. They're grinning at my success so they obviously haven't noticed the pinky-purple dampness. I do not mention it because Dominique and Arwen are too close.

All the teachers leave except one, Ms Crumpled-Crimson.

"Unhook your journals, girls," she says. "It's time to record the events of the day. Time to record your innermost thoughts."

Most pupils stay where they are but Dominique and Arwen leave our table and go and sit with a group of other red-hats on the other side of the hall. Which is a good thing.

Jess and Shalini unhook their book charms. They are both still grinning at me as the charms whizz into books. I am not grinning back. Their names are on the front. The word *Journal* is across the middle. Green leather to match their hats.

I have a book charm on my bracelet. I do not unhook it because I am pondering on whether I should tell my friends about the pinky-purple dampness and my fear that Ms Thorn will discover it before I get out of witch school with my Bottom. Maybe I shouldn't tell them. Not yet. I can't see any other patches of dampness. Maybe I imagined it? Maybe it was a trick of the light? A reflection from Ms Thorn's jacket? And the tower is miles away. Not literally. Metres?

Kilometres? Feet? Yards? Why would the broken Gellica Charm affect the walls of the dining hall? I really do think I imagined it.

Ms Crumpled-Crimson conjures up a comfy chair and plops down into it saying, "Never let anyone—"

"See your runekey," say the girls.

Satisfied, she puts her feet up and closes her eyes. She snores as if she's been asleep for hours.

Jess is covering up her journal with her arm, she's turned her spoon into a pencilspoon and she's drawing something on the cover.

"Why does Ms Rowanstall say that every single time?" she says. "Hide the runekey. Don't show the runekey as you draw it. Keep the runekey secr— What?"

Now I am doing a look from *The Book of – What?*!

"Jess! Why didn't you tell me the key to Marietta's journal wasn't a real key? I was looking for an ac-chew-al real key in the *Room of Disaster*, not a rune."

"I thought you knew—"

"How would I know!" I'm hiss-whispering. "Didn't you hear? I'm totally ignorant and not to be trusted. The journal's runekey might have been the same as the door rune but now I'll never get to test that because Marietta's book will have been wrecked by the Storm of Mayhem along with all the other books. And there might have been something useful in it. Something about Jacobus and the Gellica Charm. He knew all about the charm so maybe Marietta did

too." I sound a bit panicky. "I have to undoom the school so that I can tour my Bottom and that book might have had the answer to *all* of my problems!"

"But you *can* tour your Bottom," says Jess. "Ms Sage just said you could."

"I know. But didn't you hear the deal? I must not endanger the school! But I've already endangered the school and now I need to un-endanger it and I have no idea what to do and the pinky-purple is—"

Shalini clears her throat. She has a look on her face and it is a look from *The Book of Embarrassment*.

"What?" I say. This is becoming a very annoying and overused word.

"Well," she says reluctantly. She's twisting her skirt around her fingers. "You know. Back in the room. Everything was whizzing around and the books were flying and, well, you know, they could have actually been damaged, couldn't they, as you said, and that would have been terrible, wouldn't it? Pages could have been torn. Spines could have been broken. Covers could have been ripped right off! The books could have been totally destroyed!"

"And so…"

"Shalini!" says Jess. She says it in a voice of admiration like this. Sha-lee-nee! "Did you steal some books?"

Shalini nods and bites her lip. "Yes. A few. Maybe more. Maybe lots. Oh, I don't know! I just kept grabbing them as they flew past and putting them in my pocket. I couldn't help it."

"What about Marietta's?" we both ask.

She shrugs. "I don't know. Maybe."

*New Plan A: The Find Out If Marietta's Journal Is In Shalini's Pocket Plan will be put into operation once we have been released from the dining hall.*

*New Plan B: The Read Marietta's Journal And Hopefully Find Out How To Fix The Gellica Charm Before Ms Thorn Finds Out I Have Endangered The School Plan will follow Plan A.*

*Meanwhile: I have unhooked my book charm and Shalini is giving me a lesson in magical journal writing. On the first page I have written: This journal is the property of Twinkle Toadspit, Cauldron five, Dormitory four. Toadspit Towers, England, the World, the Milky Way, the Universe, the Cosmos.*

★

Shalini is being a very patient teacher. I am being a very impatient student because all I want to do is get to the dormitory and find out if Marietta's book is in Shalini's pocket. I am monitoring the wall situation. It has not altered. I still don't know if I imagined it.

"Clear your head," says Shalini, for the umpteenth time.

I like that word. Umpteenth. It's a Granny Wart word.

"Look at the picture," she says. She's holding her spoon up. She's changed it into a mirror so I can see myself. I look fed up.

"Remember the picture," she says. "Close your eyes and think the picture of you into your zen space. The empty space in your mind. The space of peace and harmony."

This sounds simple. It is not. My zen space is not full of peace or harmony. It is a fuzzy, foggy place of impatience.

"Then press your spoon to the page and it will

appear," says Shalini. She's been saying that a lot and yet I still have no pictures in my journal.

"Maybe you should try looking happy," says Jess. She has written two whole pages while I have been failing. "Maybe your journal doesn't want to start with a picture of doom."

"She could be right," says Shalini. "Try smiling."

I try. It is a smile of grimace. Jess and Shalini look over my shoulder into the mirror. They are grinning. Jess does the curious-eyebrow look. Shalini sticks her tongue out. Jess pouts as if she's blowing a giant kiss. I can't help it. I grin back and giggle. I close my eyes and my zen space is clear of fog. I see the picture from the mirror. It makes me laugh as I touch my pencilspoon to the page. I open my eyes. Jess and Shalini are on the page with me! I can do it!

"Now add a happy picture from your memories," says Shalini. "Just close your eyes and think of someone then add it to your zen space."

I try. It works! It's like riding a bike. Not literally. Just, once you can do it you can keep doing it. I add

Granny, Mr Marlow and Oddbod to my journal. I am about to add the entire cast of *A Midsummer Night's Dream* when Ms Rowanstall interrupts.

"Your journaling time is up, girls. Journals closed and don't forget to draw the rune to lock your secrets safe inside. And don't…"

"Show anyone your rune," say the girls together.

"Exactly," says Ms Rowanstall. "Now, off you go to your cauldrons."

This is what I've been waiting for. Now we can put Plan A into action. We beat Dominique and Arwen to the dormitory because Ms Thorn sees them in the corridor and gives them a task to do.

The dormitory is dark, there's no moonlight shining through the windows at the back, but our hats light up the seven iron cauldrons hanging from the ceiling. Dominique's is in the middle and still has the Best and Brightest rosette hanging from one of the chains, even though she is not currently the Best and Brightest so it's a lie. Arwen's is on the right, slightly behind Dominique's, and ours are set back on the left. The two spare ones are on Arwen's side, near the sinks.

We choose Shalini's cauldron because it's comfier than mine and tidier than Jess's. She drops the ladder down and we climb up. Her cauldron expands to fit as we climb inside.

The iron walls are covered in notes: spells and rhymes and chants and drawings of wee beasties and big beasties. I flop on to the mattress and duvet that fill the bottom.

"I am so looking forward to the day I can buy a mattress of softness and a duvet of fluffiness," I say. I wait for them to sit. I am watching Shalini's pocket as if the journal is about to leap out.

"OK," says Jess. "Let's find out if the journal is in there. Shalini, empty your pocket! You must comply!"

"I *shall* comply," says Shalini. She puts her hand in and says, "Fetch books!"

A book pushes its way out, forcing her hand back out of her pocket. Another follows and another and another and another. She tips her pocket upside down and lets them pour on to the duvet like a waterfall of books. She stands up and moves back to give more space. The cauldron stretches.

"I see no journal," says Jess, as the pile grows into a wonky pyramid in the middle of the cauldron. Neither do I. Soon, the pyramid is so big I can't see Jess sitting on the other side.

"That's it," says Shalini, sitting down. "My pocket's empty."

I can't spot anything that looks like Marietta's book then suddenly the books tumble towards me as Jess shouts, "Found it!"

"Yay!" That's me, from under the pile.

They dig me out and we clear a space, pushing the other books behind us. We sit cross-legged, knees touching. I put the journal in the middle, facing me, and unhook my spoon.

Shalini leans forward, hugging the rabbit I bought her as a leaving present just before I didn't leave. Jess is demonstrating overexcitement again by drumming her fingers on her knees.

"Get on with it," she says.

I hesitate. I feel like I should say something special. So I do. I put my hand on the cover.

"Greetings to you Greats-Grandma Marietta Toadspit. I thank thee for sharing thy book with me. I anticipate your words of wisdom and hope that you will help me to achieve my goal which is to—"

"Twink!" says Jess. "Just open the book!"

"If you can," says Shalini.

I wish she hadn't said that. I change my spoon to a pencilspoon. I picture the rune on the door to the secret staircase and the Gellica Charm. I draw it on the cover, underneath Marietta's name. It glows red then sinks into the leather. I think I'm expecting the pages to magically fly open with a whoosh and a flutter as if they've been stuck together for far too long and they're happy to be released. They don't. But suddenly the book grows. One second it's as thick as my thumb and the next it's encyclopedia thick. Two encyclopedias thick. Three encyclopedias thick.

"Blimey, she must really like journaling," says Jess.

I open it. The words on the first page are in a neat but spidery handwriting.

*This book is the property of Marietta Toadspit, Cauldron five, Dormitory four. Toadspit Towers, the Cross Ley, England, the World, the Universe, the Cosmos.*

"That's our dormitory!" says Jess.

"And your cauldron," says Shalini.

"What's the Cross Ley?" says Jess.

"I think it must be where some ley lines cross," says Shalini. "Maybe under the school?"

Jess doesn't look any wiser. "What's a ley line?" she says.

Aha! At last. Something I do know! "It's a magical line under the ground. Granny grows her nettles on the Fen Ley because they soak up the magic from the soil. It's why her nettle teas are so famous. They're much more powerful than any other teas. But the Fen Ley at night is a dangerous place what with the mists and the bogs and the fogs. It's where she found me when I was a baby."

I turn the page because they are both looking sad for me because I don't know why I was left in a basket all alone in the dead of night and I don't want them to be sad for me.

There's a contents page by age. I touch *My Eleventh Year*. The page turns over. There's a picture of Marietta smiling. She's pointing at her hat. She looks so happy.

"Aw," says Jess. "It's her hat day." There are more pictures. Her mother, Ursula. Her father, Henry, and six brothers: Jacobus, Griffin, Arthur, Lambert, Cuthbert and Thomas.

I flick through the pages for each year feeling quite overwhelmed by the number of words, sentences and paragraphs.

"Why did she have to write so much?" I sound fed up. I can hear it. "How can I possibly find out anything useful when there are millions of words to read?"

**13**

*Summary:*

*The New Plan A: The Read Marietta's Journal And Hopefully Find Out How To Fix The Gellica Charm Before Ms Thorn Finds Out I Have Endangered The School Plan is an impossible task.*

Jess shakes her head at me. "Twinkle. Twinkle. Twinkle. We be witches. And this," she holds up the journal, "be a magical book. So. If we want to know something. We ask it."

"That's awesome!" I say, because it is. "Let's ask about the Gellica Charm first. We need to undoom the school before Ms Thorn finds out and puts me in witch detention for the rest of my life. Because a witch in witch detention will definitely NEVER be allowed to tour her Bottom. EVER."

I obviously have no idea what witch detention would be but I'm sure it would involve complying and conforming and a complete absence of creativity. This is to be avoided.

Jess hands me the journal. "Just touch the book with your spoon and say *Witchwood, witchwood, hear my plea. Find the word* Gellica *for me*."

I comply.

The pages flick and one page sticks out from the covers. I turn it. There's a picture of Jacobus leaning against the snow globe. The title is *The Gellica Charm. Protector of the School.* Underneath it says, *Well done, Mother! The school is safe.*

That's it. It is the only page about the charm.

"Oh, dungpats," I say. "I was really hoping she would tell me a bit more than that!"

"Maybe you should ask Jacobus?" says Jess, nodding towards my pocket. "He obviously knew all about it or he wouldn't be in the picture."

Shalini gasps and stops my hand reaching for my

pocket. "No, Twink. Try searching for him first. You really need to know why he was locked in the crystal before you let him out of your pocket. If you ever do let him out of your pocket. Which you probably shouldn't."

I agree and comply. "Witchwood, witchwood, hear my plea. Find the word *Jacobus* for me."

Each page with Jacobus mentioned grows wider than the others until there's at least a thousand sticking out from between the covers. That may be an exaggeration. The first one is from *My Eleventh Year*:

*Thomas put frogs in my bed and blamed Jacobus but Mother knew Jacobus would never do that so she made Thomas jump for the rest of the day. Which was funny and really, I didn't mind. I love frogs. Not toads though.*

"Brothers!" says Jess. "Christopher once put a hot-water bottle in my bed."

Shalini and I both look at her for more information.

"It was leaking. Mam thought I'd wet the bed. He

thought it was hilarious."

The next is:

*The brothers did visit but not the oldest. Griffin and Jacobus have been apprenticed. Griffin to a silversmith and Jacobus to be a scribe for Sir Walter. Griffin sent Mother six silver runes to charm, one for each brother, to keep them safe in these troubled times. Mother allowed me to help and then she prepared a mug of hot chocolate for me all the way from the Americas. Twas my first taste. I liked it. I thanked Mother heartily in the hope I may be allowed more.*

I quickly flick through the year. "Every mention in this year is about her brother Jacobus," I say. "There's nothing about a kitten."

"Try searching for creature or charm instead," says Shalini.

I search for creature. Aha! The first mention is in *My fifteenth year.*

*Today hath been the most amazing day of my life! I have created a creature, a familiar, a cat. I am the youngest pupil to have my very own Toadspit creature to train and love. Mother said I was too young. That the creature would be immature and impulsive like me. She said she'd made mistakes when she was young and I should wait until I was eighteen like everyone else but that is three whole years away! So I did it anyway! He is purrrfect and so I must think of a perfect name! Maybe this one?*

*My first is in cat and also in bat*
*My second's in hot but never in cold*
*My third is in mouth and also in throat*
*My fourth is in many but never in few*
*My fifth is in sad and also in happy*
*My sixth is in always but never in never*
*Who am I?*

*He shall be known to all as Jacobus! I shall announce it at breakfast.*

"That doesn't make Jacobus," says Jess.

"Maybe she changed her mind," says Shalini.

I flick through some more pages. "Uh-oh. It looks like Greats-Grandma Ursula was right. Jacobus has been a creator of catastrophes and chaos since day one."

*Mother is so unfair! J turned Philomena Pumpkin into a toad for me. She deserved to be a toad because she was BEING A TOAD! And now I am to keep J on my bracelet for a week to teach him to behave. Tis a cruel punishment for he finds it constricting, like a too-tight collar on a dog. Tis the WORST punishment she can inflict.*

"Oh dear," says Shalini, as we flick through the other mentions. "He's a nightmare. Look. There's wart epidemics, dancing legs, lip glueing, storms in the dormitories, maggots in the gloop."

"Urgh! Gloop minus maggots is bad enough!" I shudder.

The list goes on as we turn the pages.

*Mother is blaming me for J's behaviour. She says he must be constrained. She says if I don't control him then he will have to be locked away. But my kitten is purrrfect. I wish I could lock her away.*

"Oh no," says Shalini. "Maybe Jacobus was controlling Marietta like he was controlling you?

Maybe that's why she cursed her mother?"

"Poor Marietta," I say. I keep turning until I reach the very last page in the journal.

*I hate Mother! No! I DETEST MOTHER!!! She hath removed my creature charm from my bracelet and locked him away somewhere. I have searched and searched but he hath disappeared! This is so unfair! Why is she blaming the witchwood blight on him? He only left the door open. He didn't know a horde of mice would invade the school and eat the witchwood. She is the WORST MOTHER IN THE WORLD!*

We are in shock! No wonder the witchwood buzzingled Jacobus! The mice are still in the school. They're still eating the witchwood roots.

"I bet he did know," says Jess.

"He's a monster," says Shalini, "You mustn't let him out, ever." She starts tidying up the other books. "Even if he does know all about the Gellica Charm."

New Plan A was a disaster. I have learned nothing useful. I have no solutions and I have a monster in my pocket. Things can't possibly get any worse.

There's a bang from the dormitory door. We hear whispering. Shalini's cauldron swings.

"Quick." Shalini pushes the books she's holding into the cupboard in her wall and gathers another pile. "Hide the books!"

Someone is climbing up.

Jess pulls the duvet out from under us and throws it over the books. It covers most. I push the rest under the pillows.

Arwen's head appears above us and then her shoulders. She looks cross. "Ms Thorn says you are to make sure you are on time for breakfast or she will double the fine," she says. "You are looking suspicious again. Stop it." Then she goes back down.

Double! That's not fair. I shall lose even more ticks that I have not yet earned.

"Time for bed then," says Jess.

We help Shalini put the rest of the books in her cupboard, which stretches to fit, but I keep the journal. We're all quiet. I climb out. Jess follows.

"Night night, Shalini," she says.

"Night night, Jess. Night night, Twink."

"Night night, Shalini. Night night, Jess."

"Night night, Twink," says Jess.

"Be quiet," shouts Arwen.

"Night night, Arwen. Night night, Dominique," shouts Jess, as she climbs up her own ladder. Dominique does not respond.

I descend into the gloom that is my cauldron bed.

14

*New Plan A: The Be On Time For Breakfast Plan has worked.*

*All other plans are non-existent and as previously mentioned I may have to resort to creative improvisation to bring The Tragedy of Twinkle Toadspit to a satisfactory conclusion.*

"As you're the saviour of the school, Wrinkle, what do you think Ms Thorn will want you to do first?" says Arwen, leaning over the table towards me. "Maybe she'll train you in magical cement mixing so you can fix all the cracks in the ceiling."

I can't help it. I look up. There are a lot of cracks in the ceiling. It may be my imagination again but there might be a hint of a pinky-purple tinge to some of the cracks. I hope it is my imagination. I look down. Arwen turns away to show her smirk to Dominique and I whisper to Jess. "Look at the ceiling. What do you see?"

Jess looks up. She gasps and then coughs to cover up the fact she's gasped.

"Uh-oh," she whispers.

Dungpats.

Jess nudges Shalini. There's another gasp and another cover-up cough.

Arwen turns back and says, "Or maybe she'll want you to produce a potion for cleaning the drains?" She gloat-eats a spoonful of blueberry yoghurt, licking the spoon clean.

Dominique is also smirking. It's a small smirk but it does exist. A little twist of the mouth, a twitch of an eyebrow. I memorise it. I have decided to memorise any interesting looks in my zen space and then transfer them to my journal in a section entitled USEFUL LOOKS FOR ACTRESSES. Thus finding

an ac-chew-al use for Dominique and Arwen's scowls, glares and sneers.

I've finished my breakfast because I did not eat breakfast. I cannot eat. I feel sick and I am exhausted. I spent nearly all night searching the book for information and solutions. I found nothing. I did fall asleep but I had a nightmare in which I was drowning in pinky-purple gloop and Ms Thorn was wearing a donkey's head and reading **Our Seven Year Plan for the Development of Twinkle Toadspit.** She was up to Year Five, the survey of the underground gloop vats, when I woke up in a sticky sweat.

I am studying Ms Sage and wondering whether to secretly tell her everything, and beg for forgiveness. She has her back to me. She's talking to Ms Lobelia at the French doors to the Toadspit Garden of Doom. Ms Lobelia teaches musical magic and nature studies but I think she should teach health and safety too because the Garden of Doom is EXTREMELY DANGEROUS! Ms Sage has yet another scroll in her hand. She passes it to Ms Lobelia, who puts it in the top pocket of her jacket of many pockets.

Sniffler, Ms Lobelia's creature that is half rabbit, half squirrel, scurries up her baggy trousers and jumps to her shoulder. He wraps his squirrel tail around her neck, trapping her bushy hair, pushing her hat sideways, dislodging some of the ivy clinging to it.

Jess nudges me. "Are you all right?" she whispers.

"I think I might *have* to tell Ms Sage before things get worse," I whisper back. "I might have to reveal all. Look at the wall now." The wall above the Boards of Embarrassment is definitely wet with pinky-purple.

I sigh. "To tell or not to tell. That is the question."

Ms Sage turns around and sees me. She calls me over. I go. I walk a *Walk of Indecision*. It is a wobbly walk with a hint of floppy feet.

"Good morning, Twinkle," she says. She's stroking Horatio's feathers. He looks like he's asleep on her shoulder. "You look rather tired. I hope you haven't been staying up late rehearsing your lines. That won't help your magical studies." She notices Ms Thorn arriving. "And Ms Thorn will want you to be bright-eyed and bushy-tailed for your training. Keep to the deal. I don't want anything to go wrong because I've decided I shall accompany you to your first performance. I am rather looking forward to seeing your Bottom again."

She gives me a cheeky smile as if she has just made a joke of great hilarity. This is my chance. She's on my side. I could tell her everything about the Gellica Charm and Jacobus and she will forgive me and fix everything and then we can make a new deal. I shall throw myself on her mercy. But first I make sure she's already sent the *Very Important Letter* to Mr Marlow.

"Ms Sage, you did send the letter to Mr Marlow, didn't you?"

"Oh my goodness, Twinkle, well done for reminding me. Horatio can take it straight way," she says. She nudges him and he blinks his eyes open.

She reaches into her pocket just as Arwen shouts, "Ms Sage! LOOK!" She's pointing above the Boards of Embarrassment.

There are shocked gasps from every corner of the hall. The wall is now leaking pinky-purple glittery water that's weirdly dribbling upwards like long, thin, pink snakes wiggling their way to the ceiling. I gasp! They're soaking through the plaster on their way to the tallest tower and the Gellica Charm!

I am doing a look from *The Book of GIANT UH-OHS!*

Things have just got much worse.

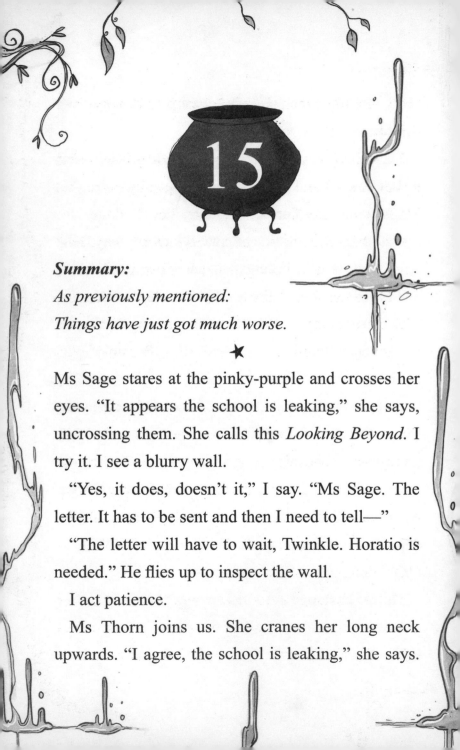

# 15

**Summary:**

*As previously mentioned:*

*Things have just got much worse.*

★

Ms Sage stares at the pinky-purple and crosses her eyes. "It appears the school is leaking," she says, uncrossing them. She calls this *Looking Beyond*. I try it. I see a blurry wall.

"Yes, it does, doesn't it," I say. "Ms Sage. The letter. It has to be sent and then I need to tell—"

"The letter will have to wait, Twinkle. Horatio is needed." He flies up to inspect the wall.

I act patience.

Ms Thorn joins us. She cranes her long neck upwards. "I agree, the school is leaking," she says.

"But leaking what, Headmistress? And why is it dribbling in the wrong direction?"

Ms Lobelia comes to investigate too. Sniffler sniffs a HUGE sniff and makes a funny squeaky noise that Ms Lobelia interprets as, "It's angelica."

I think, *gellica is an-gelica? But what's angelica?* And while I'm thinking that Ms Rowanstall pulls herself to her feet at the teachers' table. She has the look of a person who knows that something disastrous is happening. Something calamitous. Possibly even catastrophic.

"Headmistress, as the current Head of Maintenance, I have to agree with Sniffler's nose," she says. "We know Ms Toadspit infused the stones with the angelica herb as a powerful protection for the school. If the angelica is leaving the walls there could be disastrous consequences!"

Oh, dungpats. I hate that phrase.

Ms Sage's happy hat is crumpling. "Would it be fair to assume that the failure of the protection is linked to Ms Toadspit's death?" she asks Ms Rowanstall.

I answer before Ms Rowanstall.

"Yes!" I say. It's as if she's just said the most obvious thing in the world and I'm wondering why I hadn't thought it first. It's a fantastic excuse – I mean reason. "Of course it's to do with her death and deceasement because that makes so much sense and there can't possibly be any other reason, can there? Things were bound to change. The rules have gone and now so have the protections. It's obvious, really."

I'm gabbling. Ms Thorn is giving me the curious-eyebrow look as if my gabbling has prompted her to wonder if I am somehow involved in the current situation we are currently experiencing. I shut up and add the look to my other memories of looks in my zen space.

"Thank you, Twinkle," says Ms Sage. "I think it might be best if you return to your seat for now." She turns away and the teachers all huddle together whispering.

I do not need persuading. I head back to my seat but I'm almost knocked over by Ms Lobelia as she runs for the garden with Sniffler clinging to her neck. She disappears through the French doors.

I sit down. I say nothing because, as usual, Dominique and Arwen are listening. Jess and Shalini say nothing too but there is a lot of looking.

They look at me.

They look at the pinky-purple wiggly snakes of glittery water.

They look at me.

They look at Dominique and Arwen.

They look at me.

They look at the huddled teachers.

They look at each other.

Then me again.

The huddle of teachers breaks up. Ms Sage waves her hands at the rest of the pupils who have been whispering and wondering and probably worrying.

"Girls," she announces. "You must leave us. Go to your normal lessons. Horatio shall inform your teachers of the situation in the dining hall. I'm sure there's nothing to worry about."

I do not believe that statement. I do not believe that she believes that statement.

Horatio swoops over the heads of the girls as they line up. They leave as slowly as they can. They're all turning to look at the pinky-purple water that is now running up the walls like upside-down rain on a window. I get up but Ms Sage stops me.

"You must stay, Twinkle," she says. "Your friends may stay too." She turns back into the huddle of three. Ms Thorn has to bend down to hear Ms Rowanstall's whispering.

Dominique and Arwen pause too as if they are my friends. I glare at them but they ignore me and wait. I move away, pulling Jess and Shalini with me.

"Why didn't you tell?" whispers Jess.

"You could tell now," whispers Shalini.

"I was going to tell but then I thought I don't need to tell because they're blaming Greats-Grandma's deceasement for the magical mayhem and maybe they'll be able to work out a way to fix whatever needs fixing without ever knowing I had anything to

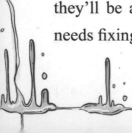

do with anything being broken in the first place. So they won't ac-chew-ally stop me touring my Bottom. It's all good."

"Twinkle." I jump as Ms Sage interrupts my whispers. She speaks quietly, seriously. "I shall be honest with you. This is a grave situation that must be resolved as a matter of urgency," she says. "Angelica leaking from the stones is a catastrophe."

I suddenly realise I am ac-chew-ally ignorant about how the lack of angelica will DOOM THE SCHOOL. So I say, "Why?"

"You are demonstrating ignorance again," says Ms Thorn.

Even though I have just used the *I* word myself, in my head, I find this statement extremely annoying and unfair. Jess and Shalini don't know either.

Ms Rowanstall explains. "Angelica protects and dispels magical threats. Ms Toadspit infused the walls of the school with angelica to ward off evil and to protect the school from the witchfinder generals that plagued our community in the seventeenth century. As long as the protections are in place the school can only be seen by those who pose no threat to the school."

Ms Sage takes over. "But now ..." she pauses and looks up at the water seeping out of the wall, "... if the angelica continues to leak, we will be visible to everyone. Friend and foe. We will be unprotected."

I hear Shalini gasp but to be honest I'm thinking, *Is that it? Is that all? That's not doom, that's not disastrous consequences! I thought the school might fall down! I thought it might explode!*

"Well, that won't be so bad, will it, Ms Sage," I say. I'm grinning with relief. "After all, Granny's a witch and everyone knows she's a witch. She doesn't have loads of protections on the cottage or the nettle fields and—"

Dominique interrupts with a look from *The Book of Scornful Looks*. "Your granny is *not* a Toadspit witch," she says.

Ms Thorn's look is from the same book. "Ms Wart is a traditional witch, Twinkle. A herbalist with a skill in therapeutic concoctions for the anxious. A hedge-witch. She does not require protections."

"But—"

I am interrupted again but this time by Ms Lobelia, who's run back from the garden. She's panting. She's definitely a gardener not a sprinter. "We're safe for now," she says. "There's no sign of any internal leaking."

"What does that mean, Ms Lobelia?" asks Shalini.

Ms Lobelia leans on Jess's shoulder. Jess sinks sideways as she answers. "Ms Toadspit didn't just protect the school from the outside threat, Shalini. The angelica prevents the plants and creatures in the Toadspit garden from invading the school."

Oh, warty boils and piles of dungpats! We *are* doomed! If the garden invades we'll all be killed in our cauldrons by scarabites and vernicious veraptors!

Then no one will ever see my Bottom again!

**16**

***Summary:***

*I am panicking.*

Ms Sage stares at the walls above the boards. "At the current rate of leakage Ms Rowanstall estimates we have twelve hours before the school is unprotected."

I push down the panicky butterflies in my stomach at the thought of the school being invaded by big beasties and wee beasties and try to think of a plan that will put everything right without anyone finding out I am the cause of the disastrous consequence. I fail.

Ms Sage unhooks a clock charm from her bracelet. She throws it at the wall behind the stage and it grows into a grandfather clock with a long brass pendulum.

It ticks and tocks. The hands are at five past nine. "We have until nine o'clock tonight," she says.

"Can't you just put the angelica back?" I say. I cross my fingers and hope for a yes.

"No," says Ms Rowanstall. "It's not that simple. The angelica must be bonded with the granite and we have no idea how Ms Toadspit achieved this. Her records are incomplete."

Ms Thorn is doing the curious-eyebrow look again. She's aiming it at me. "Perhaps Twinkle has retained Ms Toadspit's memories?" she says. "From the moment of

her death."

"I have not," I assure her. I do not like the way she is looking at my head.

"Perhaps you just *think* you have not," she says. "Perhaps they are just ... hidden."

She's looking into my eyes as if she's searching for the memories. I am suspecting she is the second person with a desire to hypnotise me. I look away.

"We should begin by understanding the problem," says Ms Sage. "Ms Rowanstall, the maintenance team and I must research. There may be something in my library. Ms Thorn, you must search the stores for angelica. Ms Lobelia, you must search the garden. Twinkle you must—"

"Come with me," says Ms Lobelia. "I will need help to carry the angelica. I have a feeling there's a batch by the west wall, if it hasn't moved or been found by the quibblers. I'll take Twinkle, Jess and Shalini to carry the plants. We'll be back in a jiffy."

She doesn't wait for the other teachers to agree. She doesn't wait for us to agree either. She tightens her belt, her tummy and bottom bulging out above and below, then strides towards the French doors. I call it *The Walk Of – Let's Do This!* Sniffler bunny hops by her side.

I am first to follow, even though it means entering the Garden of Doom and I have no wish to enter the Garden of Doom but it is better than being hypnotised by Ms Thorn, who is still staring at me as if she can see straight through my skull. I do not want her to hypnotise me and find out about the Room of Disaster and all the other things I do not want her to find out about because if she does find out about any of those things my Bottom is doomed. There has to be another way.

Jess and Shalini run after me.

We enter the garden together.

# 17

**Summary:**

*New Plan A: The Find Enough Angelica To Save The School Before Ms Thorn Hypnotises Me Plan.*

Ms Lobelia is at the edge of the garden. It's damp. She's holding Sniffler up. They are nose to nose, whisker to skin.

"Angelica, Sniffler. Sniff and seek." They rub noses then he bounces from shoulder to bottom to ground. He disappears into the plants. She turns to us.

"He'll keep popping back to let us know what he's found. Come on, girls! Grab a bag and in we go!" There's a pile of empty sacks just outside the doors. We get one each. "Just remember," she says. "Stay on the red-brick path and you'll be perfectly safe. I'm sure the protections won't have deserted us yet!"

That statement does not fill me with confidence. Shalini quickly follows Ms Lobelia as if she wants to stay as close to the safety of the teacher as possible. Jess and I walk side by side. There is just enough room if we link arms. So we do. We keep just far enough away from Ms Lobelia so she can't hear us but near enough not to get lost or swept off the path by a big beastie without her seeing.

"Now what?" she whispers.

"I'm thinking," I say.

"Have you thought of anything useful," she says.

"No. Apart from asking Jacobus for help."

"You can't possibly ask Jacobus for help!" says Jess. "You can't trust him. He might tell you to stick an angelica root up your nose and you'd do it."

"I would not. He can't control me now. My hat warns me with a tingle and blocks him. It's like a brain shield." But I do agree with her, he can't be trusted.

We keep up. Being lost in the garden is not an option. We dodge hanging leaves and odd-shaped flower heads. This part of the garden is a web of stuff like vines and creepers and ivy. It's not a jungle, it's a tangle. Sniffler returns. He leads us further along the path, squeaking for us to follow. Eventually, he stops and so does Ms Lobelia. The tangle

is too tangled. It's growing across the path. Sniffler dives in.

"Oh dear, this doesn't look good," says Ms Lobelia. "Plants aren't supposed to cross the paths."

*This doesn't look good* is not a good thing to hear in the Garden of Doom. A large orange flower that looks like a daffodil with spikes for stamens turns my way as if it's reading my thoughts. My thoughts are – *I don't like the look of that plant that looks as if it's reading my thoughts.*

"Don't be scared of the maisyheads, Twinkle," says Ms Lobelia. "They only attack if you stand on them. It's a nasty sting but what's a scar or two? We do need to clear this away though. It should not be this overgrown."

Ms Lobelia puts two fingers in her mouth and whistles. Sniffler bounds out of the tangle again. She bends down and whispers something. He leaps away again.

"I've sent Sniffler on ahead. He thinks he's scented the angelica but he's not sure. It doesn't quite smell right but we won't know why until we get through this lot. Unhook your spoons, listen and copy," she says.

She unhooks her spoon, points it at the biggest clump of roots, sucks in a huge breath, throws her head back and sings.

It's the deepest note in the history of singing!

"*Eeeeeeeoooooooowwwwaaaaaaaaaaahhhhhhh!*" She directs the noise at the path as if her mouth is a megaphone. The nearest roots and vines shrivel and pull back through the cracks in the red brick. The vibrations reach us and tickle the soles of my feet. She stops when she has no breath left.

"I call it *The Weedkiller*," she says. "Join in. *Eeeeeeeoooooooowwwwaaaaaaaaaaahhhhhhh!* The secret lies in the tone. The roots don't like the deep vibrations." She sucks in another breath. "*Eeeeeeeoooooooowwwwaaaaaaaaaaahhhhhhh.*"

"I can do this," says Jess, next to me. "Me and Mam used to pretend we were foghorns."

Before I can say, *Why would you do that?* she flicks her spoon off her wrist, drops her chin to her chest and sings.

"*Eeeeeeooooooooooooowwwwaaaahhhhhhh.*"

The vines scrabble away from the sides of the path as if Jess's voice is poison. The vibrations pass my feet and climb to my knees.

"Two ticks for Jess!" booms Ms Lobelia, looking back. She ticks the ticks in the air. They disappear. "You're a natural weedkiller!" She drags Jess to the front next to her. "Duet!" she cries.

"*Eeeeeeooooooooooooowwwwaaaahhhhhhh.*"

Jess joins in.

"*Eeeeeeooooooooooooowwwwaaaahhhhhhh.*"

As they run out of breath Jess turns back to grin at me and a blast of vibrations hits me in the chest. I quiver and shake and tremble. The trembling whizzes into every part of my body. I'm being shaken apart!

Then. Suddenly. There's an explosion in my

pocket!

Jess has shattered the crystal!

I am doing a look from *The Book of OH NO!*

Jess is doing a similar look.

"Ms Lobelia!" she shouts. "I think I've broken Twink!"

"I hope not," says Ms Lobelia. "Don't worry. This is a blame-free garden. Accidents happen. I should have warned you we never aim The Weedkiller at humans or creatures, Jess. Very dangerous. Gives them brain wobble. It can last for weeks." She lifts my chin up and inspects me. She moves my head from side to side. She seems satisfied. "Twinkle seems fine so least said, soonest mended."

I am not fine! I have a crazy cat-creature loose in my pocket. I can feel him moving about! The shape of a head pushes out against the material. I push it back and as I touch my skirt I hear him.

*Miiissttressss! Why dost thou torture me! Where is this dark? Let me out! I willst put things right. I willst comply! It's DARK!*

I let go again and he bashes against my leg. I am going to have a massive bruise where he's headbutting.

"Uh-oh," says Shalini. She's seen the pocket moving.

"What?" says Jess.

*What* is my least favourite word of the day. After *disastrous* and *consequences*. Ms Lobelia is walking away. We need to follow so we do.

Shalini moves to the other side of me. The pocket side. "You have to stop him moving," she says. "Ms Lobelia might see."

"Stop who moving?" says Jess.

"How?" I whisper back to Shalini, ignoring Jess. "I can't put him back in the crystal. It's shattered." I look at Jess in a meaningful way as I say "shattered".

"Oh," she says. "OH! OH NO!"

Ms Lobelia glances back. "Keep up, girls!"

I touch my skirt. Jacobus kicks my hand.

*Marrietta*, he yowls. *Let me out!*

I shush him and whisper, "Thou must stay calm.

Er, Mother is near. She is searching for thee. Thou is in trouble."

*It was not I!* he says, but he stops wriggling.

"Quick thinking," says Shalini. Ms Lobelia has stopped. She's waiting for us.

"Are you well, Twinkle? No after-effects of the weedkiller?"

"I'm not sure, Ms Lobelia. Do you think it will be much further? Maybe we should go back?" If we go back I can think what to do about Jacobus.

"Oh, I'm sure we're almost there," she says. "Have a sing-song, that'll speed things up."

There's a crossroads and we turn left. Ms Lobelia stops with us with a moan. "Oh no," she says. "This is a disaster. The angelica has the blight!"

There's a big patch of dead angelica plants in front of us. They look just like the plant in the snow globe, before I broke it. Grey and dried up.

Sniffler's bouncing in and out of the dead plants, squeaking in alarm. Ms Lobelia freezes then bellows, "BUZZER ALERT!!! GROUP HUG!!!"

**Summary:**

*I hate the Garden of Doom and Death! As soon as I inherit this school properly I shall dig the whole thing up and plant daisies.*

The air behind Sniffler is full of wee flying beasties. Very annoyed wee flying beasties with long pointy things on the end of their tiny noses that look very useful for stinging. Which is just typical of the Garden of Doom and Death.

Ms Lobelia hugs us. Breathing is not an option. Then, as Sniffler jumps all the way to the top of her hat with one bound, she raises her spoon and bellows, "By the power of the witchwood, by the power of the spoon, I create a bubble with the writing of this

137

rune!" She draws a rune in the air, like a stickman with his legs together and his arms waving.

There's a shimmer all around us and my skin feels clammy. Shalini's gripping my ear. I suspect fear. The buzzers are buzzing the bubble, poking with their pointy stings, trying to burst it.

Jess shouts over the noise. "That was awesome, Ms Lobelia!"

"Thank you, Jessica. It won't last forever and I can't use it again until the rune recharges, but it's better than nothing."

Ms Lobelia hugs us tighter, trapping my pocket against her leg. Jacobus wriggles and pushes and I hope she doesn't notice.

"Whatever you do, don't let go or it will burst," says Ms Lobelia. "And don't reach out to hold anything, either. That'll burst it too. This is highly unusual behaviour for the buzzers. They normally only attack on Wednesdays. Let's hope they'll get bored and fly off to find something much more interesting than us."

The buzzers are showing no sign of buzzing off. In fact, there are more now.

"Couldn't you kill them?" I say.

"What a suggestion, Twinkle! We never kill in the garden unless absolutely necessary." She says kill as if it's a rude word.

A buzzer attacks the bubble in front of my nose and I'm thinking, *But maybe this is one of those absolutely necessary moments!*

"We need to shuffle our way back to school," she says. "All together. In the same direction. Off we go."

Shuffling while holding on to other people and not bursting a bubble is not as easy as it sounds. I stand on Jess's toes, she stands on Shalini's. We all keep our feet well away from Ms Lobelia's big boots.

"Tiny steps," she says. "Keep the rhythm." She launches into song and sways from side to side as she sings, "Ten wicked witches riding on a broom, casting spells of evil, spreading doom and gloom ..."

We join in the swaying and it works.

"… un … til ... the … first wicked witch zapped the last into a frog. She zoomed off and landed in a bog. Nine wicked witches…"

Feet are saved. Toes are not stood on. Ouches are not ouched. Jess is singing the loudest. My ears hurt.

I am thinking and they are not happy thoughts. If we have no angelica then how are we going to protect the school and if we can't protect the school then the creatures of doom will invade the school and eat us for supper and then I'll be dead and a person who is dead can NEVER WIN AN OSCAR!

I am starting to wonder if the singing is annoying the buzzers and that's why they're still buzzing us. I am starting to wonder if we are not lost in the Garden of Doom when a buzzer darts at my head and its pointy sting sticks through the bubble!

"Ms Lobelia!"

Another buzzer sticks its pointy sting through, almost hitting my ear, just as Ms Thorn appears from around the next bend. For the first time ever, I am ac-chew-ally pleased to see her. She does a look from

*The Book of Surprised* and immediately points her spoon at the whirling buzzers. She says something we don't hear and they all fall dead at our feet.

"Well, really!" says Ms Lobelia. She lets go and so do we. The clammy feeling leaves my skin as the bubble pops. "There was no need for that, Constance. They would have left on their own accord eventually."

"It was necessary," says Ms Thorn. She points at the school wall behind her. "We have a school to save and we have no time to waste on sentimentality."

There's internal leaking! Pinky-purple water is dribbling up and up and up past the windows on the ground floor, the first floor, the second floor! I imagine the tower room, flooded with swirling pinky-purple water being sucked into the snow globe. It's a scene from my nightmare!

When we reach the doors I see thin thread-like roots growing into the grey cracks between the blocks of granite on either side. They are not witchwood roots. The invasion of Toadspit Towers has begun!

141

**19**

***Summary:***

*Things are even worse.*

*Ms Thorn has been told how much worse things are.*

*New Plan A: The Find Enough Angelica To Save The School Before Ms Thorn Hypnotises Me Plan has failed.*

Ms Lobelia closes the French doors. The witchwood roots surround them with thick Celtic patterns.

Ms Thorn's hat currently has more of a hessian look than a silky look. Her face, however, is blank and smooth. There is no emotion. Not even a twitch of the eyebrow to indicate a frown or scowl or alarm at how bad things are. She has resumed control of her features.

"Dominique. Arwen," she says calmly. They were waiting for her. "You will search the cellars for any type of angelica. Powdered, grated, boiled. Flowers, stems or roots. Jess and Shalini, you will join them."

"Take Sniffler," says Ms Lobelia.

"I shall inform Ms Sage of this latest development," says Ms Thorn, "and other girls will join you in your search. You may go."

Dominique and Arwen stride away as if they are about to save the school by being the first to find angelica. Sniffler jumps behind them. It looks like he's chasing them out of the hall like a sheepdog herding sheep. Jess and Shalini hang back, waiting for me, but Ms Thorn stares at them and they leave. Ms Lobelia follows them muttering something about the need for a Choir of Weedkillers.

Ms Thorn looms over me. She stands too close. "Twinkle," she says. She's looking down at me and I am looking up at her and I'm realising just how tall she is and how short I am. I have no idea what she is

going to get me to do.

"I suggest you think," she says.

"Think?"

"You are a Toadspit. You shared Ms Toadspit's memories and you have an unusual connection to the witchwood. Somewhere in your mind," she touches a pointy red fingernail to my forehead, "there may be an answer." She looks at the grandfather clock. It's twenty-five past eleven. "I fear Ms Sage's estimate was overgenerous. You do not have until nine o'clock tonight, I estimate you have only until three o'clock to discover those answers for yourself. After that, you may require ... assistance. I shall leave you to your thoughts."

I am left alone. To think. And I am thinking this.

This is all Granny's fault! If she hadn't dumped me at witch school I wouldn't have discovered I was a witch and if I hadn't discovered I was a witch I wouldn't have deceased my Greats-Grandma Ursula and if I hadn't deceased my Greats-Grandma Ursula she would still be in charge and the protections would be in place and I would still be attending St Bluebottle's School of Creativity and Fun and I would not need a permission slip signing and … Jacobus headbutts my leg … I wouldn't have a three-hundred-year-old crazy cat-creature leaping about in my pocket!

I think for what seems like hours. It isn't. A door bangs behind me. I spin round. It's Jess and Shalini. They run between the tables. They are angelica free.

"What did she say?" says Jess. "What do you have to do?"

"Does she suspect this is all your fault?" says Shalini.

She sees my face. "I mean Jess's," she says. "And yours."

"Shalini," says Jess. "This is a blame-free situation. We should focus on solutions."

My pocket is going crazy. Jacobus has obviously reached the end of his tether, as Granny would say. My skirt is flicking up and twisting around. We all watch it.

"Maybe you can trick him into helping you?" says Jess. "He's the only lead you have to the Gellica Charm. He was there, in the journal picture, leaning against the charm, and he sang the song when the rune broke. He has to know something."

"It might work," says Shalini. I am doing a look from *The Book of Surprised* that she would think that. "He thinks you're Marietta. He thinks he's in trouble. You could do a deal. You're good at deals."

The grandfather clock strikes quarter past twelve. The hall has gone darker. The French doors are now covered in tangle. Plants have planted suckers on the coloured glass, the leaves and stems are ac-chew-ally growing as we watch.

"Quick," says Jess. "Before the scarabites get in!"

I have no other ideas or plans so I improvise and comply. I undo the button on my pocket and put my hand in.

*Mistress Marietta. Meeeeoooowww.* The meow sounds sad. *Have I been punished enough now? This is worse than being trapped on the bracelet.*

I act being Marietta. "Jacobus. Thou art my creature. My anger with you hath reduced," I say. "But before I releaseth you from the darkness you must do something to help yourself. Mother thinks *you* are to blame for the protections leaking and she is seeking thee to punish thee soundly."

That just came to me. It's a good twist. Jess gives me a thumbs-up.

"And so I desireth you to impart to me the secret of replacing the gellica so that I can put things right and save you from a dire punishment. Otherwise thee will have to remain in the darkness for months, years maybe, until her anger hath cooled."

There's silence.

The room gets even darker. I light up my hat-light.

"What did he say?" says Jess.

"Nothing," I mouth.

*But thou knows the secret of the Gellica Charm,* says Jacobus.

Oh dungpats.

**Summary:**

*New Plan A: The Pretend to Be Marietta and Convince the Cat to Help Plan is not going to plan.*

"I hath forgotten it," I say. "My mind is abuzz with magical know-how. I canst not remember everything."

He's silent again.

*Release me and I will tell you*, he says.

"Tell me and I will release you," I say.

*Release me and I will tell you*, he says.

"Tell me and I will release you," I say.

*Release me and I will tell you*, he says.

"Tell me and I will release you," I say. I can keep this up for hours but we don't have hours!

The grandfather clock is ticking and the plants are creaking against the doors!

*Then I shall stay here in the dark,* says Jacobus. *Mother will eventually find out that thou hast done the deed and will punish thee not me.*

I spot a tiny grey shoot growing through the French door's keyhole. I give in. "Very well. I shall release you."

"No!" says Shalini. "Don't release the cat! He'll persuade you! He'll tongue-twist you! He'll hex you with the knee jerker!"

"My hat will protect me," I say.

"What about us!" says Shalini.

"It's OK," says Jess. "I have an idea." She unhooks her spoon and says, "Witchwood, witchwood, do the deed, be the thing that I now need." Her spoon turns into a bowl of treacle.

"How does that help?" says Shalini.

"Well. Grandma's cat didn't like being sticky and was always washing himself.

"So…

"*Step one*: Twink reaches into her pocket and grabs Jacobus by the scruff of the neck. Thus avoiding claws.

"*Step two*: She pulls him out and dunks him in the treacle.

"*Step three*: Jacobus is stuck in the sticky and is so busy licking he can't cause mayhem.

"*Step four*: He tells Twink what she wants to know so he can get clean."

I'm beginning to think that Jess does not think in the same way that other people think.

"Or I could keep tight hold and put him back in my pocket at the first sign of magical mayhem," I say.

"Or you could order him to your bracelet," says Shalini. "Like the teachers do with their creatures. Say his name and flick your bracelet. If he thinks you're Marietta it might work."

"It might." I roll my sleeve up and prepare to release the cat-creature. Undooming the school without making things worse is turning out to be quite a challenge!

Jess and Shalini back off. Jess puts the bowl of treacle on the floor. Shalini holds her spoon out, ready to change it into anything useful that will control a kitten of unreliable personality.

I put my hand in my pocket and quickly say, "Fetch Jacobus" before I can change my mind.

I feel his fur.

*Mistress!*

I seize him. I pull him out. I have him dangling by the back leg. He's a ball of fluffy white fur.

"Marietta! Mistress!" he cries, twisting round to face me. He is so cute! "Do you truly forgive your Jacobus?"

Jess and Shalini glance at each other. I think they can hear him now. I can feel him trying to control me! It's like a tickle in my mind. My hat blocks it. I act Marietta.

"I do truly forgive thee," I say. "Thou is forgiven, creature."

His tiny blue eyes grow HUGE and he launches himself at my face. I fall backwards. I let go of his

leg and he lands on my chest. He smothers me with
kitten licks and furry rubs all over my cheeks and
mouth. I cannot breathe for kitten.

"Mistress! Thou art the love of my LIFE!" he
meows. "You know this to be true. I shall be honoured
to aid you in your quest to deceive your mother and
right the Gellica Charm."

I'm thinking, *Hurrah!* But I'm also thinking, *I hate
kitten hair up my nose!*

He licks my ears, my neck, my nose, my forehead
then suddenly he jumps back to my chest. He's

staring at my hat and then at my face. His eyes grow smaller until the pupils are black and shiny and tiny.

"That hat is not the hat of Marietta Toadspit," he purrs. It's a deep purr that is a bit worrying because I can feel his claws digging into my chest and his cat breath smells of Granny's compost heap. I am not happy to see the glint of pointy teeth.

"I hath borrowed it," I say.

He ignores that. He looks around and spots the wall of witchwood dolls. He yowls, "So many witches! Why are there so many witch dolls?!"

Oh, warty boils. He knows I'm not Marietta. He knows things are different. Do I explain that Marietta's dead and he's been encased in crystal for three centuries? That's bound to be very upsetting to a cat who is obviously already living in the LAND OF NOT HAPPY and if he's not happy *and* upset he may not want to help us. Plus, there is also the possibility that he may go all ninja cat and claw me to shreds with the claws that are digging through my shirt. So telling him this must be avoided at all costs.

"Puss," says Jess. She holds her fingers out as if she has a tasty titbit. She lies down, stretching out on the floor at right angles to me. "Puss, Puss." He watches her warily. "I'm afraid Marietta's dead and you've been encased in crystal for about three hundred years."

Oh, dungpats.

His claws dig deeper. I shush Jess. She ignores me.

"But Twinkle here," she points at me, "has just let you out. She's a Toadspit. She's the only Toadspit in the school since Ms Ursula Toadspit went deceased. Look, she has Ms Toadspit's bracelet. You're hers now. You *muuuusssst* obey her or it's the bracelet for you."

She lifts my wrist up and jingles the bracelet at him. His claws prick my skin, which hurts, and he purrs, "I do not have a Mistress Marietta? No one knows my name?"

"We do," says Jess. "It's JACOBUS. JAC-O-BUS."

"Of course it is," says the kitten. He yowls and I

think he's yowling for Marietta but he's laughing. He leaps off me and starts jumping around like a kitten chasing sunbeams. "No Mother to moan. No Mistress to pander to. No bracelet of torture! I am truly free!"

He yowls another laugh then he stiffens and his ears prick up. He glances towards the French doors. He meows a warning. I twist my head to see what's there.

Oddbod is there. Standing on the witchwood roots. He hisses and the witchwood roots shudder. They twist and writhe and squirm into thorny patterns.

Jacobus hisses back. He keeps his eyes on Oddbod and sings.

"Three blind mice, three blind mice, see how they run, see how they run, they all run after the witchwood tree, they nibble the roots of the witchwood tree, they gobble the roots of the witchwood tree, three blind mice. Meeeeooooowwww!" It's a laugh. A taunt. He's sneering at Oddbod!

Oddbod leaps across the hall towards the kitten.

Claws out. This is not good! I flick my bracelet and say, "JACOBUS!" in a commanding voice.

He laughs and suddenly spins from a fluffy cat into a silver charm.

Jess throws the treacle but misses as the Jacobus charm shoots up leaving a silvery trail through the air. He disappears into a crack in the ceiling. He does not hang from my bracelet.

"Uh-oh," says Jess. Oddbod is covered in treacle. "I think we just made things worse."

**21**

*Summary:*

*Things are definitely more worse than when they were worse last time they were worse.*

*New Plan A is now: The Capture The Cat So That Ms Thorn Does Not Discover I Have Endangered The School And Stops Me From Touring My Bottom Plan.*

*New Plan B is now: The Reverse the Leakage So That Ms Thorn Does Not Discover I Have Endangered The School And Stops Me From Touring My Bottom Plan.*

*Or they may be the other way round.*

Shalini pulls me to my feet.

"I said, *Don't follow the voice!*" she says. "I said, *I have a bad feeling about this!* I said, *No good comes of secret staircases!* And I said, *Don't release the cat!* And now, things are worse than they were!"

"But you said he would go on the bracelet!"

"I know!" she says. "And now I feel like it's all my fault too because you might not have released the cat if I hadn't said that!"

"I would just like to remind you both that this is a blame-free situation," says Jess. She's cleaning treacle out of Oddbod's ears.

I am puzzled though. "But why wouldn't he go on my Toadspit bracelet? I said his name. I flicked my wrist."

"Maybe it has to be Marietta's bracelet?" says Jess.

"I hope not," I say, "because we have no idea where *that* is."

The kitchen door bangs open and Ms Lobelia marches in followed by a line of witches. It's a mixture of teachers and pupils. They all have their witchwood spoons in their hands and a look of bravery on their faces although some of the younger girls look terrified.

"Jessica," bellows Ms Lobelia as soon as she spots us. "Join on the end." She marches towards the garden. It's a *Don't Mess With Me March*. She throws open the doors even though they are now completely covered in plants, takes a deep breath and blasts them.

"*Eeeeeeeoooooooooowwwwaaaaaahhhhhhh.*"

The plants retreat. She attacks. She is marvellous.

"I think I want to grow up to be Ms Lobelia," says Jess. She runs outside and joins in with the Choir of Weedkillers forcing their way through the tangle. They spread out and the last witch closes the doors behind her, muffling the noise.

"That's one problem solved, then," I say to Shalini. "We're safe from the Garden of Doom."

"You are mistaken," says Ms Thorn, from behind me. "This is a temporary measure. The witches will

tire. Their voices will weaken. They will need sleep and the destructive plants will return. We require a solution to the core problem. You have had time to think, time to access your shared memories. Do you have the means to protect the school?"

"I do not," I say. I have nothing. No ideas. No important memories.

"That is unfortunate," says Ms Thorn. "I shall speak to Ms Sage. You will be hypnotised. Felix is adept at this skill."

Fangus, whose real name is Felix, but Fangus suits him better, stares his tiny batty eyes at me and they grow like swirly lollipops.

This is a moment of declaration, so I do declare. I stand up to do it. "Ms Thorn. I refuse to be hypnotised by a bat!"

"The choice is not yours to make," she says. "The school must be saved."

I am about to reply that there is always a choice and I choose *no* but I am interrupted by a bell ringing. Girls appear from every doorway, except the garden, obviously. Ms Sage bustles in and takes to the stage. She hurries everyone.

"Come along. Come along. You *must* sit down at the back!" She doesn't wait for them to comply.

"I have to inform you that we have made no progress. No progress whatsoever," she says. She looks cross and her hat's turned dull and floppy. Some of the lace has untangled. "We have found absolutely no angelica, the protection is still leaking and it's speeding up but we must eat. Food feeds the mind as well as the body and we all need to think." She's looking at me.

I do think. I think, *Stop looking at me.*

"Eat quickly and return to your year group teachers. They will assign your tasks. Cat ash must be collected by those not involved in saving the school. Not a single cat must die because of this tragedy."

"I hadn't even thought that was a possibility!" I say to Shalini.

"They can't regenerate in the witchwood if we don't collect the ash," she says with a worried look.

Ms Sage jumps off the stage with a flurry of floaty silk and velvet. She smooths it down and sits at the teachers' table with a knife and fork at the ready.

Ms Brewbody brings in the floating trays as Dominique and Arwen arrive. Sniffler bounds outside to Ms Lobelia and they hurry over to report to Ms Thorn. They obviously haven't found any angelica either. They sit with us. They do not engage in conversation.

Food is flying on to tables when an orange-hatted girl at the next table stands up and points at me. She has black curly hair and green eyes but there are tiny sparkles of blue in each.

She launches into a loud song. "Twinkle, Twinkle, little star, how I wonder what you are, witchy fool or witchy brat, how much power is in your hat?" Then she gives the most enormous sneeze, *ATISHOO!* and sits down looking quite puzzled at her own behaviour.

"That was odd," says Shalini.

"As is Twinkle," says Dominique.

"She's not odd, she's unique," says Jess, plonking

herself down. Her chair creaks. "We've cleared a space all along the side of the school. Should give us time to eat before we have to clear it again."

"Where are the others?" says Shalini.

"They were behind me," says Jess, just as a green-hatted first year runs in screaming.

"The Slumberous is coming! The Slumberous is coming!"

**22**

**Summary:**

*I suspect a Slumberous is a bad thing.*

The rest of the Weedkiller Choir race in. They're tripping over each other.

"It's behind us!"

"It's behind us!"

"Barricade the doors!"

"It's behind us!"

Ms Lobelia is last through. She slams the French doors shut and shouts, "These will never keep him out! I need tables! Man the barricade!"

We all jump up. Tables are dragged as questions are asked.

"Who woke the Slumberous?"

"Why would he wake now?"

My question is, "What's a Slumberous?" My other question is, *Why do things always have to get worse?!*

"I don't know," says Shalini, which is quite surprising because she is my go-to source of information on all of the Toadspit Tower beasties, big and small.

Arwen ac-chew-ally chooses to explain. So she can feel superior.

"Legend has it the Slumberous is a creature gone wrong. It was Ms Toadspit's first attempt at creating her own familiar. It sleeps among the roots of the witchwood tree, feeding on the sap. It's been asleep for over three hundred years and it should not be awake now. It should not wake, ever."

Ms Lobelia booms, "Did someone aim the *Weedkiller* at the Slumberous?"

"It was not me!" says Jess, as Dominique aims a glare at her. "Plus, blame-free dining hall," she adds.

Panic fills the hall. Witches are dragging tables over to barricade the door. Cats jump out of the witchwood roots. They're purring the flutey-purr they purred when the witchwood saved me from the Toadspit Terrors. Oddbod's pulling at my skirt, meowing at me. I reach down to stroke him and he grabs my thumb in his mouth, pulling me towards the witchwood roots. I'm fizzingling.

Suddenly I know how I can save the school from the Slumberous!

I dodge in and out of the tables and panicking girls with Oddbod at my heels. Ms Lobelia is leaning another table across the doors and Ms Sage and Ms Thorn are organising the stacking of the tables. The flagstones in front of the door are shaking. I'm suspecting the Slumberous is big. Possibly even huge. Possibly even gigantic!

"Stay back, Twinkle!" shouts Ms Lobelia, tipping another table against the doors.

I ignore her. The tangle outside is shaking. Whatever a Slumberous is, it's coming closer!

I press my thumb into the witchwood roots and say, "Witchwood, witchwood, hear me plead, give us now the help we need. Protect the witches from the Slumberous, that is so big and very …" I can't think of a rhyme! "… lumberous! Make this hall a safer space and keep them safe within this place."

My thumb fizzingles a fizzingle of happiness as the connection flows. Oddbod purrs and the cats join in. The purring is soothing and everything slows down as golden lines whizz along the roots like flashes of energy. Tiny threads grow like spider silk across the glass. They grow thicker and weave in and out of each other like threads ... weaving. The roots stretch across from both sides. They touch. They twist. They lock.

My hat is twirling around my head, splashing colour across the shadows. I am an ac-chew-al witch of mega power! I am the seventh of seven! I am the Toadspit of Toadspit Towers! I feel the power! I am the power! I pour the power into the witchwood.

Thousands of spidery web threads grow out of the new roots. They touch. They twist. They lock. Grow. Touch. Twist. Lock. It only takes seconds and the door is covered.

Ms Lobelia drops the table she's about to add to the barricade. Ms Sage claps her hands and Ms Thorn does another look from *The Book of Surprised*. I am ac-chew-ally copying that. Being a witch of mega power is awesome!

The witchwood keeps on growing. It spreads across the wall on each side, covering the stones in a layer of witchwood roots. My thumb is hot.

There's a huge bang and we all jump. It

sounds like the Slumberous has used a battering ram against the French doors. Or its head. Or maybe its bottom. I have no idea which bit of its body it's using because I have no idea what a Slumberous looks like! Then there's a bellow like a hundred bulls bellowing and I'm suspecting it looks ENORMOUS!

Glass cracks. The witchwood thickens. It spreads up, following the upward drips of angelica still seeping from the stones. It spreads sideways, into cracks, across the Boards of Embarrassment, across the dolls and the doorways. It's making a witchwood cave out of the dining hall.

I watch it cover the entire hall. My thumb is still connected but my hat has stopped shining. I feel sleepy. Dizzy. Powerless. As the witchwood covers the last block of granite I close my eyes and slump to the floor.

23

**Summary:**

*I might be dreaming.*

I'm a feather drifting through the air. Not literally. I'm *like* a feather. I'm like a drifting, twirling feather, probably from a parrot, that's falling towards a fluffy white cloud that makes me think of the duvet of delight in the Toadspit Catalogue. I drift into the cloud. It surrounds me. I would LOVE to own a duvet this comfy. A great big ginormous duvet all warm and snuggly and...

"We could slap her." It's Jess. Someone is rubbing my hand. I'm suspecting Shalini. I open my eyes. It is. She smiles.

"You've been asleep for over an hour," says Jess.

An hour! "But that means—"

"Time's running out," says Shalini. "The protections will soon be gone."

"And Ms Sage hasn't sent Horatio with my permission slip!" I've woken up to a nightmare.

Shalini shakes her head at me as if I have my priorities all wrong. "I think it's time to tell," she says.

I try to sit up but can't. I was not dreaming this bit. I am ac-chew-ally wrapped up in an ac-chewal duvet of delight and I am lying on a mattress of comfort. Oddbod is sitting on my legs.

I'm trapped in a corner of the dining hall, blocked in by two tables tipped on their sides. It's like being in a cot. Shalini and Jess are inside with me. Everyone else is outside. I peep through the crack between the tables. Some of the pupils are huddled in the centre of the room, they're sneezing and looking sorry for themselves. The rest are sitting at the tables looking worried. The teachers are pointing witchwood spoons at the witchwood-coated walls and chanting.

"What are they doing?"

"You've trapped everyone in the hall," says Jess. "The witchwood won't let anyone out. Of any door."

"So they're trying to get the witchwood to release us," says Shalini. "Because no one can fix anything while they're trapped in here."

Oh, dungpats! This is a catastrophe!

"But that's not what I meant it to do."

"We guessed that," says Jess. "Also, Ms Thorn has decided that the only solution to everything is to hypnotise you as soon as you wake up."

Oh, dungpats! No.

"I am doomed. I've made things worse AGAIN!"

There's a huge sneeze from one of the huddled girls.

"That's been going on a while," says Jess. "And sometimes they break into—"

"Twinkle, Twinkle's fast asleep." It's a yellow-hatted girl in the middle of the huddle. She's standing on a chair and singing loudly. There's a blue flash in her eyes. "In her dreams she's counting sheep. In her mind time's spinning round, there is no answer can be found. Twinkle, Twinkle's fast asleep. In her dreams she's counting sheep. ATISHOO!"

"It's Jacobus," says Shalini. "He keeps swapping from one person to another."

Arwen sneezes.

"You must face away from I when you sneeze!" shouts Dominique. "You must stay away from I! You must join the other diseased girls."

"But it was just a sneeze," says Arwen. "I didn't say a rhyme. I think I'm getting a cold." She sneezes again. "See," she says.

I can't help it. I laugh. So does Jess. Dominique and Arwen not-getting-on is comedy.

Shalini shakes her head at us. "It's not funny," she says but there's a little smile trying to get out. "We have to put this right."

"Starting with what?" says Jess. "Fixing the school? Which we do not know how to do. Catching Jacobus? Which we do not know how to do. If only we had a way to find out what Ms Toadspit knew. If only we knew someone who had all those memories in her head. If only we—"

I can see where this is going. "You are not hypnotising me."

"But, it's the only way," says Jess. "Either I do it, or Ms Thorn and Fangus will. Or you can tell Ms Sage everything."

I can't tell Ms Sage everything! She hasn't sent the permission slip.

The witchwood roots creak and the hall shudders as the Slumberous batters the doors again.

I give in. "OK. You can do it."

"Uh-oh," says Shalini. She's peeping over the desks. "Ms Thorn's looking over at us. I think she might be coming... Yes, she's setting off."

"We have to get out of here," I say. I think fast. I lift Oddbod off my legs. "Oddbod, please delay Ms Thorn. Stop her coming over here."

Oddbod understands. He leaps over the table and runs across to the teacher. He gets in the way, meowing around her witchwood leg. The leg starts tapping and it turns her round.

"Right," I say. "Escape Plan A coming up. The nearest door is in the doll wall but there are some teachers trying to open a way through it. Step One: Someone must distract those teachers."

Shalini looks at Jess. So do I.

"That would be me then," she says. She pushes the table away from the wall and strides over before I can say, *ready*, or *steady*, or *go*. She stops in front of them and sings really loudly, up close. "Twinkle, Twinkle is my friend. Even though she's round the bend. I love her and she loves me. Like a diamond in the tree. Atishoo! Atishoo!"

The teachers back away. Jess sings louder.

"Twinkle, Twinkle is the best. She is better than all the rest. Atishoo! Atishoo! Atishoo! Atishoo!"

They back away even further. It's working!

"Twinkle, Twinkle, is my— Oh!" Jess shudders. Her eyes flash blue. She looks at her wrist. There's a new silver charm dangling from her bracelet.

## 24

**Summary:**

*GIANT PATS OF DUNGPATS! JESS IS JACOBUS!*

"Shalini! Jess is a Jacobess!"

Jacobess dances. She spins round. "Ring-a-ring o' roses, we've all got dribbly noses. Atishoo. Atishoo. We all fall down!" She falls over. The huddled girls fall over too. "Witches in the dining hall, don't know what to do. Atishoo! Atishoo! Boo, hoo, hoo!"

The hall is filled with crying and sneezing girls and teachers trying to work out what's happening as they usher them towards the huddle in the middle. There are more girls in the huddle than out of the huddle. It's only the girls who are affected, not the teachers.

"Poor Jess!" says Shalini. "What if he stays on her

bracelet?"

"I think he's gone, look."

Jess sits up. Her eyes are green again. She's looking around, confused, dazed and scared. She sneezes. She sneezes again. She sobs and pushes herself backwards into the doorway and curls up there all by herself.

"What if he goes back on?" says Shalini. "And what if once he's been on your bracelet he can make you do things without being on your bracelet?"

"Why would you think that?" I say. "That's a bad thing to think."

"Because he can't be on *all* of *their* bracelets, can he?" she says, pointing at the huddle of girls.

"Oh, dungpats. Today is turning into the worst day EVER. It can't possibly get any worse." I really must stop saying that!

"Uh-oh," says Shalini. "Ms Thorn's on her way again. No. Now she's talking to Ms Sage."

"Keep an eye on both of them. It's time for Step Two." I quickly think of a rhyme and connect my thumb to the roots behind me. "Witchwood, witchwood, do the deed, make for *us*, the space *we* need. Between the wall and wood *we'll* hide, then towards the door *we'll* slide." I use the picture of the three of us from my journal as a zen space picture so the witchwood will know who to hide.

A gap opens up.

"Uh-oh," says Shalini. "She's coming!"

"Quick! In." I push her into the gap. She squeezes along. The witchwood twists and turns to let her through and I quickly squeeze in next to her. We freeze as the witchwood closes over us. I can see Ms Thorn through the tiny gaps in the knots. There's a determined look about the way she's walking towards our corner. As if the moment has come to delve into my brain whether I am asleep or not.

She reaches my cot. She peers over the tables. She is definitely doing a look from *The Book of Extremely Surprised and Amazed*, which is the sequel to *The Book of Surprised*. I suspect she has lost her ability to maintain an expression of nil emotion. She looks around the hall but she does not see us. She does not see Jess either, she's disappearing behind the witchwood into the doorway.

Shalini and I do not move until Ms Thorn has turned away. Then we slide sideways. Going slowly so no one notices two witch-shaped bulges moving across the witchwood wall. We reach Jess. She sneezes.

"Horrible," she says with a sob. "Horrible. Horrible. Horrible."

I don't waste any time reassuring her because time is ticking away. As I think that, the grandfather clock strikes twice. Two o'clock! I have one and a half hours left to fix this and get my *Very Important Letter* to Mr Marlow!

I picture an open door with us going through it. "Witchwood, witchwood, hear my plea, open for my friends and me."

The door behind us flies open and Jess falls backwards. We drag her into the corridor and the door shuts.

She is still dazed. She's rubbing her head and

shaking it.

"What should we do with her?" says Shalini. "She can't hypnotise you like this."

Jess looks at us blankly as if she can't hear us. She sneezes again.

"We need to get her away from here," says Shalini. "We need to hide from Jacobus until she's recovered. Come on."

We pull Jess up. Her legs are wobbly. I help her to walk as we follow Shalini along the corridor. We stop at a broom cupboard.

"In here," says Shalini. She pushes all of the brooms to the back and we sit Jess on the sacks.

"Cracks!" says Jess. She's running her hands over the walls and pointing at the ceiling. "Not safe. Cracks! Charm! *Atishoo!*"

She's so pale, I'm beginning to worry. I am beginning to think going back and telling all to Ms Sage is a good idea.

"Bubble," says Jess. "Bubble. Bubble. Bubble."

"Jacobus has broken her brain," I say. "she's

babbling."

"No," says Shalini. "She wants a bubble. That's a great idea!" She pulls us close so our legs are touching then lifts her spoon above our heads. "By the power of the witchwood, by the power of the spoon. I create a bubble with the writing of this rune." She draws the stickman rune in the air. A bubble forms over all of us. I am impressed.

Jess shakes herself, like a wet dog. The colour comes back into her cheeks and she blinks. She blinks some more. And some more.

"I think the bubble's cutting off the connection to Jacobus," says Shalini.

"Urgh," says Jess. "That was disgusting! He's a monster cat! There was a zap on my wrist, like a shock, and then he was inside my head. Making me say stuff. Making my body move. He totally controlled me. Then, when he whizzed off my bracelet, it was like he left a little bit of himself inside my mind, like a shadow. So I would keep sneezing. He's mean." Her normally cheerful face is no longer cheerful. "We have to stop him!"

"Maybe Greats-Grandma Ursula will tell us how," I say. "I'm ready, if you are."

"I am definitely ready," says Jess. She gives herself another shake then flicks her spoon off her bracelet and into her free hand.

"Witchwood, witchwood, do the deed. Change to be what I now need." A silver watch and chain twizzles round her fingers until they are tied together. "Make yourself comfortable," she says to me. "You have to be relaxed."

I lie back on a pile of sacks. Shalini moves to the side, keeping contact.

"So," I say nervously. "How many times have you ac-chew-ally done this?"

Jess twizzles the chain back the other way and releases her fingers. "Let me think," she says. "There was the 'finding Grandma incident', and the 'lost leg incident', then there was the 'missing cucumber incident'. But that was Mam hypnotising me, so that one doesn't count." She stops.

I wait. She doesn't say anything else.

I sit up. "So. Two."

"Well, yes, two. But I know what I'm doing. It's really just about getting you to enter a sleepy state. Then your mind does the rest. Lean back and take three deep breaths."

I comply and she begins to swing the watch.

"Good luck," says Shalini.

"Look at my watch," says Jess. "Follow the watch," she says. "Watch the watch," she says.

"Stop the spooky voice," I say.

"But it's—"

"No," I say. She gives in.

"Watch the watch of shininess," she says, in her proper voice but it's slower and deeper. "See the silver, swishing and swinging and swishing and swinging." Her voice is going even deeper. "Let your eyes swing and swish with the watch. Let your mind rest. Let your body relax. Swing and swish and swing and swish…"

My body is ac-chew-ally relaxing. Maybe this is because I'm still tired from using all my power to save the school and the fact it has been a really, really busy day and I think, *Wouldn't it be nice if I could just fall asleep now and wake up to find this has all been a dream and there was no such creature as Jacobus.*

My eyes are following the swishing and swinging, left and right and left and right and left and right … they cross. I still see the watch. It's in my zen space.

The empty space between my ears. The swings leave behind silver streaks, like speeding car lights on a dark night. They fill my zen space. They spread, they go further into my mind. Like trails of silvery silken memory threads.

25

I have the strongest feeling that the threads lead to memories. I pull on one. Nothing happens. I wonder, in my floaty state of relaxation, if I should say what I'm looking for. Like in the journal. I tug another thread and think, *Protect the school.* Nothing happens. I tug again and think, *Fix the school.* Nothing happens. I tug. I think, *Ursula Toadspit.* I think, *gellica.* Suddenly lights spin along the threads. Faster and faster. Images flood my brain. Too fast to see. Too fast to hear. Too fast to memorise.

I am jolted out of my floaty state of relaxation.

"Quick," I shout to Jess. "I need paper. I need a pen!"

Jess says, "Fetch paper." She pushes it into my hands. Shalini gives me a pen. I scribble as the memories flood through my fingers and on to the paper. I draw until my mind is blank and my zen space is empty. I drop the pen and close my eyes. I am exhausted again. Magic is very tiring.

"There you are," I say. "The answers are on that paper."

"Does this actually mean anything?" says Jess. She pulls the paper from my fingers.

I open my eyes and frown at her. Questions are not appropriate. Does she not realise I am mentally exhausted! I have just been through an experience of brain overwhelm.

"Is it some sort of code?" says Shalini, squinting at my drawings.

I take the paper back.

"Of course it means something," I say. "I've drawn almost every single memory that whizzed through my brain." I look at my scribbles and drawings.

Oh, dungpats! They do not make any sense at all. I turn them around. They still don't make any sense. I have drawn memories over memories over memories. Layers of memories.

"I think I see a giraffe," says Jess.

"And there's a pineapple," says Shalini. "And a balloon, with eyes and a moustache?"

"I think that's actually a caterpillar," says Jess.

I can't believe the hypnotism has failed. I think I did secretly hope that it would give us at least one clue. I drop the paper.

"Now what?" says Jess. "We don't know anything that we didn't know before. And that was nothing."

"And we're running out of time," says Shalini.

"All of the angelica will be gone soon, the beasties and the plants will invade and we'll be eaten down to our bones by the scarabites! I think the time has come, Twink. We have to tell Ms Sage everything. If we take her to the secret room maybe *she* can find a way to fix the leak. Fix the snowstorm. Maybe even reverse it. Then *she* can deal with Jacobus."

Jess nods. "Sorry, Twink, but I agree with Shalini. We can't fix anything. We're only first-year witches. We should tell."

I can't believe they are giving up even though I was ac-chew-ally, just at that moment, thinking that maybe we should give up.

"But if we tell then that's it. Career over. It won't just be my Bottom I don't get to tour, none of my other parts will be performed either!" I make a very sad face. This is not acting.

"Not everything is about your Bottom, Twink," says Shalini. "Sometimes other things have to come before Bottoms."

"Sometimes Bottoms have to come last," says Jess.

They are attempting humour to cheer me up but it's not working. Gloom is descending because they are right. Death by scarabite is not a death anyone should experience. Not even Dominique or Arwen. I shall accept my destiny, which is obviously to be trapped at witch school forever and never win an Oscar. One day someone will write about this tragedy of a wasted acting life.

"Twink?" It's Jess.

"I GIVE IN!" That's me. "I'll tell Ms Sage everything but not when Ms Thorn's there. Or Dominique. Or Arwen. Let's go." I pull my hand away from Shalini but Jess holds me.

"Stop! What if Jacobus is out there?" she says. "We can't burst the bubble."

"I'm not going to burst the bubble," I say. "I'm just trying to get up."

"Do you want this?" says Jess. She's holding up the paper with the overlapping memories. She pushes it closer to my face. Too close. She's touching my nose. My eyes cross. Suddenly the drawings split into layers, like layers of tissue paper. I am like Ms Sage! I am *Looking Beyond*! I see things I couldn't see before. I push and pull on the layers. I bring some to the front, push others behind. I make connections I couldn't connect.

I grab the paper. It ac-chew-ally does have the answers to EVERYTHING!

"We have to go," I say. I throw the door open and run out. I go left.

"Twink!" cries Jess, chasing after me. "You've burst the bubble! You said you wouldn't burst the bubble!"

Shalini shouts, "And that's not the way to the dining hall!" as she joins in the chase.

"I know!" I cry. "It's the way to the *Room of Wonderful Things*!"

"But why are we going to the *Room of Wonderful Things*?" says Shalini.

"And why is it *Wonderful* and not *Disastrous* now?" shouts Jess.

I run faster and shout back.

"Because I know how to put the angelica back into Toadspit Towers!"

## 26

***Summary:***

*New Plan A is now: The Put The Angelica Back Into Toadspit Towers Plan.*

*New Plan B is now: The Wow Ms Sage With My Super Saving Of The School Plan.*

*New Plan C is now: The Get Ms Sage To Send Off My Very Important Letter Plan.*

*New Plan D is now: The Solve The Problem Of Jacobus Plan. This does not yet exist.*

"I was an idiot! We don't have to fix the school. We just have to fix the snow globe! Come on!"

"Stop!" cries Jess. "We need to make another bubble of safety."

"We can't run in a bubble of safety!" I shout back. "And I need to run! I need Ms Sage to send the permission slip! Deidre Kemp is waiting in the wings with her Bottom at the ready!"

Shalini catches up. "I knew we'd end up back in the *Room of Wonderful Things*!" she says. "I just knew it."

"I think we all did," says Jess, from my other side.

We run up the creaky stairs.

"What if he's following?" says Jess. "He could be in that crack. Or that crack. Or that crack. Or—"

I ignore her. I feel like I have a clock ticking in my chest, not a heart. It's ticking away my chance of stardom.

"Slow down!" gasps Shalini.

"Can you hear him?" says Jess.

"No."

"What about now?"

"No."

"What about now?"

She is driving me crazy!

"NO!"

Shouting does not stop her asking. She asks all the way to the secret door. She asks while I search the wall and press the rune to open. She asks as the stones slide apart. I step in. They follow and we start the climb. The steps are a bit slippery with pinky-purple.

"What about now?" says Jess, directly behind me.

I do not answer. Talking is not an option while a person is run-climbing on slippery steps. I can hear her gasping as we reach halfway. My leg muscles are crying out for me to stop and I name the steps *The Steps of Torture*.

Eventually I follow the curve and see the door. The wind is still howling behind it. Thick pinky-purple watery streams are snaking their way out of the stones and under the door.

Jess staggers on to the landing. Shalini follows.

I don't wait. I fling open the door and I jump in.

Ac-chew-ally, I'm sucked in. We're all sucked in to a freezing pinky-purple snowstorm. We grab hands. Our fingers are already icy and our breath is coming out in clouds of steam.

We fly around and around the massive gellica plant in the middle of the room. The dark-pink stem is as thick as a tree trunk and the umbrella flower head is a mass of purple flowers. The shelves are empty. All of the soggy books, scrolls and artefacts are whooshing round in a whirlpool of angelica with the plant at the centre.

"What's the plan?" yells Jess, over the howling pink snowstorm.

"Do we need to find the snow globe?" yells Shalini.

"No!" I yell back. "Not yet! We have to reverse the storm with the gellica tree song that Jacobus sang! We have to put the angelica *into* the school, not *out of* the school. Join in!!"

I start. "Here we go round the gellica tree, the gellica tree, the gellica tree! Here we go round the gellica tree on a cold and frosty morning! We spin the gellica *into* the school, *into* the school, *into* the school. We spin the gellica *into* the school on a cold and frosty morning!" They join in. The spinning plant slows down.

"It's working! Keep singing! Here we go round the gellica tree, the gellica tree, the gellica tree! Here we go round the gellica tree on a cold and frosty morning!"

We sing until my throat goes dry. We don't stop.

The whirling snowstorm slows and slows and slows. We drop down towards the whirlpool of books and our toes dip into the pinky-purple as it stops whirling for a heartbeat. Then it spins and spins and spins the other way and we're lifted up again.

"Yay!" shouts Jess. "We're doing it!"

"Look out!" cries Shalini. "Books!"

The heavy leather-bound books spin up and away from the pinky-purple whirlpool. They fly towards us. Missing our heads. Artefacts flash past. I'm hit by a spider statue, right in the stomach. I let go of Jess and Shalini.

"Don't stop singing! We spin the gellica *into* the school, *into* the school, *into* the school. We spin the gellica *into* the school on a cold and frosty morning!"

I kick a silver horn. I duck under a book. I dodge. I catch. I dodge a golem. It shatters on the wall behind me.

"Oh no!" shouts Shalini. "We have to save the artefacts! They haven't been catalogued!"

Jess changes her spoon to a tennis racket. She bats a boot at my head.

"Catch them in your pockets," she shouts. "Then they won't get broken!"

I open my pocket wide and use it as a net. I catch as much as I can. Shalini does the same. Jess hits to me, to her, to me, to her.

A scroll to me.

A book to her.

A necklace to me.

A bracelet to her.

"You're amazing, Jess," shouts Shalini.

"I take after Mam," shouts Jess.

I glimpse the base of the snow globe through the whirlpool as it empties but I'm still blinking away the stinging needles of snow and it disappears under a wave of pinky-purple.

"Make a circle again!" I yell. "Here we go round the…"

I grab Jess's shirt. She grabs Shalini's. Shalini grabs mine. We are spinning together.

"Closer!"

We tighten the circle until we're in a hug spinning above the plant. It's shrinking as the angelica pours back out, like sweat. It soaks into the walls. Sparkles in the stones. We cling to each other and spin until the wind drops and our feet touch the floor. It's damp and clear of books around the broken snow globe. The plant is small, grey, and dead on the base. The snow is swirling around it. Not us.

I bend down and push the two halves of the rune on the base together. They're black. I twist them, there's a click and the rune turns red.

The room is suddenly quiet, apart from the noise

of dripping. The air around the plant glistens and twinkles, like a sheet of tiny stars. It forms a globe and covers the plant, turning to glass. We watch the snow swirl around the stem and the dried flower head until it settles to the bottom.

I do not believe it!

A Plan A has ac-chew-ally been completed! We all sigh a sigh of success and exhaustion. We all smile the smile of happiness. We all hug the hug of congratulations! We all …

… hear something.

We hear…

"Meeeooooww!"

I dash over and touch the shelf. My thumb buzzingles.

"He's coming!"

Jess runs. So does Shalini.

The Jacobus charm swirls out of a crack. There's a flash of silver and a flurry of white fur in the air.

I run too.

Jacobus's meowling laughter chases me out of the door. He's singing, "Little Twinkle Toadspit, fixed the Gellica Charm. Worked out the trick and kept the school from harm. She doesn't know the trick of me, she doesn't have a clue, I can hex and curse the girls, there's nothing she can do! Meeeeooooowww!"

He is right! Which is so annoying. We run, jump,

slip and stumble down the steps, all the way to the door. I push the rune and we're out! I press to close and the stones slide back into place. We all lean against the wall. Breathing fast.

"We did it!" gasps Shalini.

"We be witches!" says Jess. Then she starts to giggle. She infects Shalini and she infects me and for a moment I wonder if Jacobus has infected us with a giggle hex but then Jess stops and wipes her eyes on her shirt sleeve. I do too.

"Right," I say. "Now we go to the hall and show Ms Sage the protection is back, release everyone from the witchwood cage, get Ms Sage to send off my—"

"*Very Important Letter*," say Shalini and Jess with a few more giggles.

I grin.

"Nothing can stop *that* happening now. And then we deal with Jacobus."

"How?" says Jess.

"I have no idea," says I.

"Twink!" Shalini sounds excited. "I might have something that can help."

I run down the corridor.

"Tell me later," I shout back.

"But Twink, I think I've found—" she shouts. But I don't wait. I can't. the grandfather clock is ticking away my chance to perform my Bottom.

I beat them back to the dining hall. The witchwood cage is still in place. I pay my respects and ask it to make a doorway. It does. I step through just as the clock strikes three o'clock. There's still time!

The angelica is dribbling down not up, behind the witchwood, soaking back in to the walls. I touch the witchwood again. "Witchwood, witchwood, the task's complete, please shrink back, depart, retreat."

Happy fizzingles fill my thumb, spread along my arm, up my neck and into my hat. I do the happy dance.

The last roots to grow, on the ceiling, are the first to retreat. They twist and unwind, shrink and shrivel.

I'm not sure anyone's noticed my arrival amid the

TOTAL CHAOS that is the dining hall. It's noisy and busy with witches testing spells, chanting, and arguing loudly over which rhymes will work. It's smelly with fires burning under cauldrons of potions and concoctions.

Jess and Shalini come in behind me.

"Look!" says Jess. She's twirling round. "The roots are changing."

The huddle of sneezing girls in the middle of the hall is bigger and the sneezing is louder. Ms Sage and Ms Thorn are at the garden end of the hall with their ears pressed against the witchwood barricade.

Ms Lobelia has her arms folded and a cross look on her face. She booms at Ms Thorn, "I am absolutely certain the Slumberous has gone, Constance. I felt him leave. How could you not feel the pounding of his feet going away?"

I hug my friends. "It's ac-chew-ally working. I am the *Saviour of the School*! I shall wow Ms Sage!"

"Twink," says Shalini. She's fiddling with her pocket. "I—"

"Not now, Shalini," I say. I walk across to Ms Sage, Ms Thorn and Ms Lobelia. I am doing the *Walk of Success*. This is a smooth walk, a confident walk, a back straight, arms swinging, relaxed walk. I match it with a look from *The Book of Victory* because the school has been saved and now Horatio can deliver my *Very Important Letter* and I will get to Tour My Bottom. My look changes to a look of excitement.

Oddbod sees me and runs over. He walks by my side like a guard dog.

The teachers have not noticed my walk or my arrival. I cough. They turn around.

Ms Thorn is doing a curious-eyebrow look. A *Where exactly have you been?* look.

So as not to give her an opportunity to speak first, I speak first. "Ms Sage, Ms Lobelia, Ms Thorn." I nod to each. "The Slumberous has indeed gone and I would like to draw your attention to the latest development in the ongoing saga I like to call *Toadspit Towers: All's Well That Ends Well*."

I point upwards with a dramatic flourish. I indicate the angelica soaking back into the walls. They all gasp, even Ms Thorn. I am pleased with this response. It bodes well, as Granny would say.

"I give you the final act. The protections have been restored."

I allow them a moment to take this in. Ms Lobelia laughs and it's the best and biggest laugh I have ever heard. Ms Thorn's curious eyebrow is so high it's disappeared under her hair. Ms Sage is clapping her hands like a baby seal. The walls are sparkling through the witchwood.

"As you can see, Ms Sage, the school has been saved so if you could just ask Horatio to deliver my *Very Important Letter* I can help to tidy up before tea time." It's possible this will earn me some ticks and

I think, *PIES*!

"Is this your doing?" says Ms Sage to me, clasping her hands to her heart. She has amusement in her smile again.

"It is," I say. "I have ac-chew-ally saved the school." Then I suddenly think, *OH NO! I have not thought this through! She's going to ask me how I saved the school and then Ms Thorn will work out that it was all my fault in the first place and she'll insist I endangered the school and broke the deal! My Bottom is doomed!*

"How?" says Ms Sage. As I just predicted she would! I think fast.

"I would love to tell you the tale of the saga of how I saved the school, Ms Sage. Perhaps I will write a play and perform it for you, but first, you *must* ask Horatio to deliver my *Very Important*—"

I am rudely interrupted by Dominique.

"Ms Sage! STOP! Twinkle Toadspit is not the *Saviour of the School!*"

**28**

*Summary:*

*I AM LIVING IN THE LAND OF SHOCKED!*

Dominique is holding the Gellica Charm. How can she be holding the snow globe? She points a finger at me. "Twinkle Toadspit is a fraud!"

I hear Jess and Shalini gasp behind me. I gasp too. My gasp is the loudest. I do not believe what I am seeing! And hearing.

"Whatever do you mean, dear?" says Ms Sage. She's looking at Dominique over her glasses.

Dominique smirks at me. It is a very expressive smirk. A superior smirk. If I wasn't so cross and confused I would memorise it for my journal.

She raises the snow globe above her head like a

trophy. "I give you … THE SNOW GLOBE OF GELLICA! The charm that hath protected the school for over three hundred years. Broken by the incompetent Twinkle Toadspit and repaired by *I*. The Best and Brightest in the school!" Her brown eyes flash with blue.

"Twink!" hiss-whispers Shalini. "Dominique is Jacobus. Jacobus is Dominique. She's a Dominiqobus!"

Oh dungpats! She's right. I can see the Jacobus charm on her bracelet!

Dominiqobus sees me seeing the Jacobus charm on her bracelet. She smiles a smile of superiority.

"The broken snow globe was discovered by *I* in the tallest tower of Toadspit Towers," she announces to the entire room. "A tower that has been locked since the death of Ms Ursula Toadspit."

She holds the snow globe higher.

"The Gellica Charm was repaired by *I*."

She holds it even higher.

"The gellica was returned to the stones by *I*."

She can't possibly lift it any higher.

"You may all applaud the Best and Brightest witch of the school!"

She turns slowly so that everyone can see the globe.

Some of the girls applaud. Not the sneezy ones. Arwen does confused clapping. The slow, hesitant sort.

"Twinkle," says Ms Sage. "Is this true? Have you lied?"

I cannot speak. I do not know which words will get me into trouble and which words will get me out of trouble so I am

SPEECHLESS! Oddbod rubs his head against my leg as if he senses my confusion.

"Twinkle?" Ms Sage is being insistent.

It's all gone wrong. My career is over. I am doomed. I might as well tell Ms Sage everything.

"That is not Dominique Laffitte!" I say. "That is a ... crazy cat-creature from the seventeenth century!"

"The child has gone mad," says Dominiqobus. "She should be punished."

She comes closer. She whispers her words in my ear.

"Pussycat, pussycat, where have *I* been? Locked up by a witch, for being so mean. Pussycat, pussycat, why am *I* free?"

She grins and steps back. It's a slow grin like she's making me wait for the next bit.

"Because, you think *I* am him, and don't know I am me!"

She laughs. It's a laugh with a hint of yowl.

"Perhaps Ms Thorn should take that from you, Dominique dear," says Ms Sage. Ms Thorn takes the snow globe. Dominiqobus doesn't object. "Please take the Gellica Charm to my office for safe-keeping Constance. We shall study it as soon as I have dealt with this situation. Ms Lobelia, see to the girls. They may leave now that the witchwood has opened the doors."

Ms Thorn looks like she'd rather stay to observe more of my humiliation, but she complies and starts to leave as Ms Lobelia ushers Shalini and Jess towards the sneezing girls. They do not want to go either. Shalini is still trying to tell me something and I am now wondering what it is but Ms Lobelia gets in the way.

"Oh, but thou *must* let everyone stay," says Dominiqobus in a cute kitten voice. "Oh, please, I beg of thee, Ms Sage." She's not really begging. "They be such fun to play with. Look at that one. The silly-looking one with the freckles and the red hat." She points behind me. Ms Sage looks surprised. I turn around. Dominiqobus is pointing straight at Arwen.

"Dominique!" says Arwen. She's looking hurt and very, very puzzled.

The Jacobus charm spins with a flash of silver from one wrist to the other. Dominique slumps down on to the nearest chair with a huge "*ATISHOO*" and Arwen stands up, points at me and sings.

"Eeny, meeny, miny, moooo, Twinkle doesn't have a clue. Cannot know the name that's true. Eeny meeny miny mooooo!"

Arwen's nose grows a big boil on the end. She screams and faints. There's another flash. Another boil grows on another girl's nose. She screams and faints too. Then another and another. Jacobus is spreading a boil epidemic! Ms Lobelia drags the infected girls into the huddle.

Dominique stands up straight again. The charm is spinning on her bracelet.

I notice Ms Sage noticing the charm. She frowns. Then she smiles her smiley smile of persuasion at Dominiqobus. That's a brilliant idea! I hope it works.

"You *must* sit back down, Dominique dear," she

says. "You have just saved the school. You *must* be tired."

"I prefer to stand," says Dominiqobus.

Oh dungpats.

Dominiqobus smiles a smiley smile of persuasion at Ms Sage. "*You must* take a seat," she says.

"I also prefer to stand," says Ms Sage. "But you *must* sit. I insist."

Dominiqobus does not comply. She continues to smile at Ms Sage. It's a smile that says, *Make me*.

# 29

**Summary:**

*It's a magical standoff.*

Ms Sage continues to smile her smile of persuasion. Dominiqobus continues to smile hers.

Ms Lobelia is handing out hankies to the sneezing girls. Jess stops her and reaches up to whisper something. Ms Lobelia looks across at us as Jess whispers some more. Ms Lobelia frowns. Shalini joins them and she whispers too. Ms Lobelia nods and she whispers something to Ms Thorn and then the nearest girl. They hold hands and that girl passes the whisper to another girl. The whisper passes like a virus around the hall.

I try not to watch in case Dominiqobus sees me

watching because then she might wonder what Jess is up to and try to put a stop to it whatever it is. Luckily, she's still challenging Ms Sage to a smiling duel.

Dominique, dear," says Ms Sage. "I'm not sure you're feeling yourself today. I *must* insist that you obey me."

"Witch," says Dominiqobus, she's undoing her tie as if it's too tight. "You may cease your efforts to control me. I can no longer *be* controlled. Or constrained." She pulls the tie off. "Or trapped. Not even by an *ignorant* Toadspit." She throws the tie in my direction.

They both look at me. Ms Sage is frowning. Dominiqobus is gloating. Oddbod jumps up into my arms. He looks from me to Dominiqobus. He meows.

Not the *I* word! Not again. I am not ignorant. I know everything about Marietta's cat-creature. I stayed up all night and read every mention of his name in the journal, not that he knows that. If there was a secret to controlling him then Marietta would have written it. Maybe I missed something? He keeps dropping clues because he's convinced I can't defeat him. I try to remember them.

*You think I am him, and you do not know me? No Mother to moan, No Mistress to ... something. No bracelet to torture. And ... no one knows my name!*

But he has a name. He's Jacobus. Marietta named him Jaco— Oh!

*Twinkle doesn't have a clue. Cannot know the name that's true.*

Jacobus is not called Jacobus! That's why he thinks no one can control him! Marietta was the only one who knew his name.

Ms Sage tries again. "I *insist* that you *must* be tired, my dear."

Dominiqobus laughs a meow.

"Nay, witch. I be wide awake," she says. She is amused by Ms Sage's attempts at control. "I feel the need for sustenance. Bring me fish. Salmon. Fresh and juicy salmon. And milk. Warm milk. Or shall I infect more girls?"

Suddenly Ms Thorn raises her spoon and shouts,

"By the power of the witchwood, by the power of the spoon. I create a bubble with the writing of this rune." A bubble immediately surrounds every girl and teacher holding hands. The sneezing and crying stops instantly.

Dominiqobus whirls round. She's doing a look from *The Book of I'm Very Annoyed.*

Jess and Shalini are outside the bubble. Why are they outside the bubble! Shalini's fiddling with her pocket again. Why is she fiddling with her pocket when they should be safe in the bubble of safety! What exactly is she trying to find?

"Oh, well done, everyone," says Ms Sage. "That was quick thinking."

I need quick thinking too! I hug Oddbod and close my eyes. I snatch at a memory. I pull a silver thread in my zen space. It tugs and I tug back, thinking *Who am I?* A page from Marietta's journal whooshes into my brain.

*My first is in cat and also in bat*
*My second's in hot but never in cold*

*My third is in mouth and also in throat*
*My fourth is in many but never in few*
*My fifth is in sad and also in happy*
*My sixth is in always but never in never*
*Who am I?*

I guess. The first letter is a C or an A or a T. That's enough. I tug at the memory of the brothers' pictures. If Marietta named Jacobus after one brother, then his real name might be a brother too.

Cuthbert. Arthur, Thomas.

"*ATISHOO!*"

I open my eyes. Jacobus has left Dominique. She's dropped to the floor and he's whooshed into a cute and cuddly fluffy kitten. He's prowling and purring towards Jess and Shalini. Jess has a tennis

racket thrust in front of her and Shalini has her hands behind her back. She's hiding something.

Oddbod leaps out of my arms and jumps over the tables to land between the cat and my friends. Tis a moment to act.

"JACOBUS," I project my voice. It is a voice of authority and ownership. "Jacobus. Jacobus. Jacobus."

He pauses. He turns around. His little black cat mouth is smirking.

This is a hands-on-hips moment, so I put them there.

"I am Twinkle Toadspit, the seventh of seven, wearer of the Rainbow Hat of Awesomeness and bearer of the Witchwood Charm. I *own* this school. I own this table. This chair. This floor. This wall."

I'm being Jess!

"I own *thee*. I am your mistress and thee *will* obey me."

"I obey no one," meowls Jacobus. "Not now." He turns the threatening purr on me.

I see a silver glint out of the corner of my eye. Shalini has thrown something shiny into the air. Jess bats it at me. She shouts, "Twink!" I catch it. It's a bracelet. Jess is mouthing something. *Marry a yeti.* Marietta's! The bracelet is Marietta's!

I act an evil laugh. "Ha ha ha ha! Now I have you, cat-creature!"

I dangle the bracelet from my fingertips. The points of the knitting-needle charm are as sharp as claws.

"Dost thou recognise the fabled bracelet of Marietta Toadspit … Jacobus?"

I suspect he does because he backs away.

"Thee *will* obey me … Jacobus. For I *own* thy bracelet and I *know* the secret to controlling thee … Jacobus. Or should I say … Cuthbert!"

I flick the bracelet.

# 30

*Summary:*

*Oh dungpats.*

Nothing happens. He does not whizz into a silver charm. He does not spin to the bracelet. He yowls a laugh.

"Twinkle, Twinkle, that's not right! On thee a twisting tongue I smite!"

My tongue twists. It's like a snake in my mouth! A wriggling, wiggling, twisting snake. I do not like it.

I try to say Arthur.

It comes out "Farfler."

I try to say Thomas.

It comes out "Whomath."

But Jacobus reacts! There's a flash in his eyes.

It's Thomas! His real name is Thomas! I smile even though my tongue sticks out. He sees the smile. He does not like the smile.

"Thomath!"

My hat twirls.

"Whomass!"

My hat lights up.

"Thomasth!"

Jacobus hisses. "Twinkle, Twinkle, cease thy speech—"

My hat fizzingles!

"THOMAS!"

I flick the bracelet. It snaps like a whip. Jacobus yowls, "No, Missssstressss! I will be gooooo—" But it's too late. He whizzes from fluffy kitten to silver charm and suddenly he is spinning on the bracelet.

Trapped.

His blue eyes flash and then turn silver.

There is stillness in the hall for a second.

Then Ms Lobelia bursts the bubble of safety over the girls and starts clapping. "Thirty points to

Twinkle, the Saviour of the School!" she cries. She is my favourite teacher!

The girls applaud and cheer and throw away their hankies. I assume they're applauding me so I take a bow. Then I curtsey. And bow again. I am prevented from continuing by Jess and Shalini, who have wrapped themselves round me in a giant hug. Ms

Sage is clapping her sea lion clap and showing no signs of stopping. Jess and Shalini release me.

I hold the bracelet out to Ms Sage and wait for her to stop. She does.

"Ms Sage, please allow me to introduce you to Jacobus, secretly known as Thomas. Marietta Toadspit's creature who was locked in crystal three hundred years ago and released by me but only because he made me do it with the Power of Persuasion. So it was not my fault and this is a blame-free situation and I cannot be blamed for any magical mayhem or catastrophic consequences that resulted from any of my actions." I glance at Ms Thorn as I say that bit. She does not respond.

I hand over the bracelet to Ms Sage. She inspects the charm.

"Are you telling me that *all* of today's magical mayhem was actually caused by this creature?" she says.

I consider that question. I answer.

"Yes."

Because tech-nic-ally that is correct. If Jacobus hadn't lured me up the stairs I wouldn't have followed the noise and Jess wouldn't have knocked the globe off the books and I wouldn't have clicked the rune and released Storm Mayhem. Therefore, this answer is, obviously, not a lie.

"He was discovered in the tallest tower of Toadspit Towers, through a secret door. I would be delighted to take you on a tour of the tower and explain all but before I do, as I am not to blame for disrupting the school, endangering the school, or interfering with the smooth running of the school … please will you allow Horatio to deliver my letter?"

I point at the grandfather clock.

"It is quarter past three."

Ms Thorn interrupts. "Perhaps an inquiry should be held, Headmistress," she says. "Before rewards are given."

The boards click. Ms Lobelia's points are added. The four for being late yesterday are taken away. Still not enough for a duvet. But plenty for pies!

"Oh, I don't think an inquiry is necessary before rewarding bravery, Constance," says Ms Sage, and another thirty ticks click on to my board!

She takes the letter out of her pocket and Horatio swoops on to her shoulder. She puts the letter in his beak and whispers into his owly ear. He flies off, disappearing through one of the windows above the balcony without opening it.

"There we are then," says Ms Sage. "You shall tour your Bottom, Twinkle, and I shall look forward to seeing it."

I am smiling a smile of happiness!

31

**Summary:**

*This is the current situation I am currently experiencing in my current location.*

*I have spent my ticks. I am lying in my cauldron bed wrapped up in a duvet of fluffiness. I have eaten pies. Sticky, drippy, dribbly cherry pies of deliciousness. I am officially stuffed. AND I have had an idea of genius! I have turned my spoon into a mattress of comfort and I am currently living in the LAND OF COSY.*

*My pocket is empty, so is Shalini's, and our cupboards are full of artefacts and books from the* Room of Wonderful Things. *Ms Sage does not know about*

*these. She only knows about the things that were left in the room. She is beyond excited but Ms Thorn is still insisting on an official inquiry.*

*The letter was delivered and I had a reply. So all I have to do now is keep out of trouble for two weeks and then I can get out of witch school and the Tour of My Bottom shall begin! That's fourteen sleeps! Nothing can go wrong now!*

# Acknowledgements

This book was written with the help of chocolate. Chocolate bars, chocolate buttons, chocolate eclairs, chocolate liqueurs, choc ices and truffles. Sometimes, on extra tough writing days, there was added fruit and nut, salted caramel, ginger, chilli, almonds, sea salt and toffees.

Less calorific help was supplied by my amazing editor, Kirsten Stansfield, at Nosy Crow. Kirsten very calmly talked me through what was working and what wasn't working at each stage until we had a book that we were both happy to release into the wild. Thank you also to Fiona Scoble and everyone involved in producing the finished book: designers, marketers and PR gurus. You are wonderful to work with.

One of the highlights of being published with Nosy Crow is being teamed up with illustrator, Jamie Littler. It is such a special moment when I get the first rough drawings and see my characters coming to life with such humour. The book feels real at that point, so big thanks to Jamie for being able to visualise what's in my head!

My thanks also go to my agent, Amber Caraveo, who has helped to keep me on track and answered all my questions patiently, even the daft ones.

The SCBWI gang have continued to be awesome with their advice for a newbie, their online support and their enthusiasm for my writing. You really are a fantastic group of friends and colleagues.

Last to be thanked again, but first in every other way, my family. They haven't quite got over their excitement at the launch of *You Can't Make Me Go To Witch School* and now they have to cope with another one! The biggest thanks goes to Geoff for providing the chocolate, the day to day support and the love.

Readers – If you have laughed as you've read this book then Twink and I are DOING THE HAPPY DANCE!